the BOOK CLUB Boyfriend

New York Times & *USA Today* Bestselling author

KENDALL RYAN

The Book Club Boyfriend

Copyright © 2025 Kendall Ryan

About the Book

She doesn't believe in love. He doesn't believe in losing.

Let the games begin.

Scarlett "Scottie" Calloway built her career writing books about why women *don't* need men. Romance? *Overrated*. Soulmates? *A marketing ploy*. The last thing she wants is to spend a summer co-hosting a romance book club with an arrogant, insufferably handsome hockey player who thinks he knows a thing or two about love. *Immediate no*.

Chase Remington lives for three things: hockey, winning, and pushing Scarlett's buttons. He's never met a challenge he couldn't charm his way through—until her. The queen of anti-romance loathes him, and frankly? He's having the time of his life getting under her skin.

But when a PR stunt forces them together, their battle of wits turns into something far more dangerous—an attraction neither can afford. She swears she won't fall. He bets she will.

By summer's end, only one will be right.

And if there's one thing they do have in common?

Neither likes to lose.

1

THE ESCAPE PLAN

Scarlett

There's nothing more ironic than a woman who writes about how much better life is without a man… sitting alone on her couch, eating peanut butter straight from the jar, and spiraling.

Not that I'm spiraling.

I'm *contemplating*. Deeply. Existentially. Like one of those tortured, brooding artists who chain-smoke on their Parisian balconies and stare moodily at the rain—except I live in Dallas, it's ninety-seven degrees outside, and my balcony overlooks an aggressively mediocre parking lot.

Also, I look like a dumpster raccoon.

My hair is in a half-fallen bun, I'm wearing a ratty old sweatshirt that says *Love is Dead* across the front (which, at the time of purchase, felt both on-brand and hilarious), and the only thing I've accomplished today is discovering that if you eat enough peanut butter, your jaw actually gets tired.

All of this would be fine—comical, even—if I had *written a single damn word today.*

But I haven't.

Not yesterday, either. Or the day before that.

In fact, the last thing I wrote of substance was last year's *empowerment masterpiece, How to Die Alone (and Love Every Second of It)*, a bestselling manifesto on why women don't need a soulmate to be happy. That book had my signature tone—sharp, insightful, delightfully scathing. It was everything my readers wanted from me. Everything my *publisher* wanted from me.

And now?

Now, I am *failing* to deliver.

I push the jar of peanut butter onto the coffee table with a frustrated sigh and stare at my laptop screen like it personally betrayed me. The cursor blinks. Taunting. Mocking.

There was a time when I could churn out chapters effortlessly, weaving together the kind of biting, liberating truth bombs that built my entire career.

It all started when, after a bad breakup, I wrote a blog post that went viral about the lie that is modern romance (*If He Wanted to, He Would, But He Doesn't, So Move On*) and became a full-blown cultural phenomenon. Three bestsellers. A TED Talk. Daytime talk show circuits. Women in my DMs, thanking me for helping them walk away from toxic relationships.

I *thrived* on it.

Thought I was actually doing something good in the world.

But now?

I blow out a breath, glaring at the open document on my screen—working title: *How to Want Nothing and Get Everything.*

It was supposed to be my next big hit. The kind of book that reinforces my brand, secures another multi-six-figure deal, and further cements my reputation as the woman who doesn't need a man, thank you very much.

Except... the words won't come.

And I'm terrified to examine why that is.

I squeeze my eyes shut and shake the thought away because *absolutely not.* This is what burnout looks like. A minor blip in my creative genius.

I just need inspiration. A fresh setting. A change of scenery.

Which is exactly why I'm escaping to Michigan for the summer.

It was Harper's idea—my best friend, my agent, and the only person who gets away with calling me out on my bullshit. She practically packed my bags for me, saying I needed to "unplug and get out of my own head" before I snapped and wrote something so unhinged it would permanently tank my brand.

So, I'm going.

To a quiet beach town.

Alone.

And if all goes according to plan?

I'll come back recharged, re-inspired, and ready to write another *iconic* takedown of love and its false promises.

But first?

I'm going to wallow for at least another hour because even a self-sufficient, independent woman is allowed to have a dramatic moment before she figures her life out.

The second I step out of my car, the wind off the lake rushes over me—cool, crisp, and carrying the unmistakable scent of water and freshly cut grass. The air tastes different here, cleaner somehow, with that mineral tang that only comes from the Great Lakes. Beneath my feet, the gravel driveway crunches, still damp from morning dew. In the distance, I can hear the rhythmic whoosh of waves against the shore, punctuated by the cries of gulls circling overhead. The late afternoon sun filters through the massive oaks, creating dancing shadows that remind me of being thirteen again, watching this same light play across my mother's face as she laughed on the porch.

I close my eyes, inhale deeply, and *finally* feel like I can breathe again.

This is *exactly* what I need.

A break. A reset. A summer of solitude in a charming beach town with a rental house that, based on the listing, is basically a Pinterest dream.

I open my eyes, and yeah—this place is *glorious*.

A charming white cottage, tucked between towering oak trees, with a wide front porch that practically demands you sit and drink coffee in an oversized sweater. But the *real* selling point? The sprawling back deck that faces the lake, perched high enough to give a perfect view of the endless blue horizon.

It's breathtaking.

I pop open my trunk and grab my suitcase and duffel, but before I can drag them up the porch steps, my phone buzzes.

I groan. I already know who it is before I check.

"Harper, I literally just got here," I answer, tucking my phone between my ear and shoulder.

"*And?*" she demands, like she's been holding her breath waiting for an update.

For the love...

I glance around, taking in the quiet, the stillness, the absolute *peace* of it all. "I hate to admit it, but… you were right. It's perfect. Just like I remember."

She makes a triumphant noise. "I *told* you. You need this, Scottie. You need to unplug, get out of your own way, and let this place *heal* you."

I roll my eyes. "Okay, that's dramatic."

"I'm serious! You've been in a *creative death spiral*, and frankly, I'm terrified of what you'll write if you don't take a second to recalibrate. Like, I don't know, a manifesto on why everyone should commit tax fraud instead of dating?"

"That's not *entirely* off-brand for me."

She groans. "Just *relax*, okay? Swim in the lake, read something for fun, do *not* go on a weird feminist rage spiral about love—"

"I don't rage. I *educate*."

"Scarlett."

I sigh dramatically. "Fine. I'll relax. Maybe even be one of those *chill* people who post scenic Instagram stories with captions like *just vibes*."

"You *are* a writer. Maybe *write* something?"

"Hey, I have every intention of—"

"Not something *angry*."

I scowl. "I don't *only* write angry things."

Harper hums like she doesn't believe me, and okay, *fair*.

I've built an entire career on cynicism. But for the first time, I don't know if I want to *keep* writing the same thing.

I shake the thought away.

"This place *does* feel… nostalgic," I admit, kicking a rock by my foot. "The last time I was on this stretch of beach was the summer before my parents' divorce."

Harper softens. "You were happy there."

I nod, throat a little tight. "Yeah. I was."

There's a pause, like she's debating whether to push further, but Harper knows me well enough to let me sit with that thought.

"Well," she finally says, "if anything can shake the creative cobwebs off, it's that lake air. I fully expect you to be barefoot and having a spiritual breakthrough by week's end."

I snort. "I'll settle for just getting *one* decent chapter down."

"And no men. No distractions. You *promised* me a summer of self-care."

I scoff. "Trust me, I'm not about to start craving male attention out of nowhere. I'll be in full-on hermit mode."

Harper makes a satisfied noise. "Good. Call me if you need anything. And if you don't send me at *least* one sunset picture in the next twenty-four hours, I'll assume you've been kidnapped and murdered and call the authorities."

I smirk. The sunsets over the lake are glorious. "Understood."

I hang up, shaking my head as I shove my phone in my pocket.

No distractions. No men. No drama.

Just me, my laptop, and the perfect setting to write my next bestseller.

What could *possibly* go wrong?

2

THE OFF-SEASON PLAYBOOK

Chase

The off-season is supposed to be *relaxing*.

It's supposed to be the time when I get to kick back, sleep in, hit the golf course, hang with my bros, and not think about anything other than which beer to crack open first.

Instead? I've got team management breathing down my neck, a contract negotiation looming, and a PR problem that apparently needs *solving*.

I rub a hand down my face as I lean against the kitchen counter, staring at my phone. The screen is lit up with notifications—texts, DMs, a few missed calls.

A handful of them are from the team. My agent. A reporter I definitely do *not* feel like talking to.

And a few? A few are from women whose names I probably should have saved but didn't.

I *could* text one of them back.

It would be easy. Mindless. A distraction from the weight pressing against my ribs, the quiet frustration I can't seem to shake.

Instead, I sigh and push my phone aside.

"Looks like it's just you and me for the summer, bud," I say, glancing down at my dog, Rip. He blinks up at me, completely uninterested in my personal crisis, before flopping onto the floor with a sigh.

I smirk, bending down to scratch behind his ears. "You'd make a terrible therapist, you know that?"

He thumps his tail, then immediately rolls onto his back, demanding belly rubs.

I shake my head. "Needy."

Not that I can talk. My team's been on my case about this whole *marketability* thing since the playoffs ended. I get it—I really do. The Stampede want a captain they can slap on billboards and use in commercials, and apparently, my reputation still screams *reckless playboy who doesn't take anything seriously.*

It doesn't matter that I haven't been that guy for a while now. The narrative has already been written, and if I want that letter sewn on my sweater next season, I need to change it.

Fast.

I grab my keys and pat Rip on the head. "Be

good. Try not to eat the couch again."

He yawns in response.

I roll my eyes and head out, ready to meet Bennett for a beer. Maybe I'll get some actual *advice* from the guy, considering he managed to turn his whole image around last year.

Or, at the very least, maybe he'll buy the first round.

When I arrive at the bar, I immediately spot Bennett at a high-top table near the back, nursing a pint and watching me like he already knows I'm in a mood.

"Look who finally decided to show up," he calls, smirking as I drop onto the stool across from him.

I scowl. "Relax, *Dad*. I'm, like, three minutes late."

Bennett lifts his beer. "Three minutes *closer* to me watching you spiral over this whole 'grow up and be responsible' thing."

I grunt, waving down the waitress for my own drink. "I'm not spiraling."

"Right." He takes a sip. "That's why you look like you just found out Santa isn't real."

I flip him off, and he grins.

"Let me guess," he continues, clearly enjoying himself. "The team's on your ass. Your agent won't stop calling. And somewhere in that cluttered brain of yours, you're wondering if sleeping with the head of PR would just make this all go away."

I snort. "That last part *isn't* true."

Bennett raises a brow.

"…Probably."

He laughs, shaking his head. "Look, man, this isn't complicated. You want to clean up your image? Show the team you're leadership material? Do what I did. Play nice with the book club crowd."

He's talking about *The Stampede's Romance Book Club*—a ridiculous PR stunt that turned into a *thing* two years ago. What started as a way to make the team more marketable to female fans ended up blowing up in the best way possible. The league ate it up, the fans *loved* it, and Bennett—who was supposed to be the face of the whole operation—went and fell for Lucy Quinn, the snarky sports blogger who gave him hell at every turn.

Now, once a month, a group of professional hockey players get together to *seriously* discuss romance novels with the readers, complete with livestreams, viral memes, and more fan engagement than the damn Stanley Cup Finals.

It *should* be embarrassing.

But somehow? It's *not*.

And worse? Bennett's right. It did wonders for his career.

The dude's an absolute golden boy in the league now. Practically walks on water.

I scowl. "Yeah, well, I don't *need* some fake

PR romance book club to fix my rep," I mutter, taking a sip of my beer.

He smirks. "You sure? Because it would do wonders for your dating life."

I scoff. "My dating life is fine."

He levels me with a look. "Dude, your dating life is a *rotating door*."

I glare. "It's the *off-season*. I should be able to have *some* fun without it being a scandal."

Bennett sighs. "Look, I'm just saying—you're a great player. But the team wants more than that from you now. You've been around a couple of years. They want a guy who can lead, who can represent the franchise." He lifts a brow. "You really gonna blow your shot at captaincy because you can't stop being *you* for five minutes?"

I open my mouth, then shut it.

Damn it.

I hate when he makes *sense*.

I rub the back of my neck, annoyed. "I just need to get out of Dallas for a bit. Clear my head. Figure out what's next."

Bennett leans back, intrigued. "Where you headed?"

"Michigan." I exhale, already picturing it. "Grew up outside of Grand Rapids, spent summers on the lake. I rented a place there for a month. Should be quiet, no distractions. Just me and Rip."

"*No distractions*," Bennett echoes, smirking.

"You? Alone? With nothing to do but *think*?"

I scowl. "I *can* be alone."

He chuckles. "Sure. Just make sure you don't go full existential crisis up there. I don't want to get a call saying you've abandoned hockey and opened a bait shop or something."

I roll my eyes. "I'll be fine."

Bennett hums. "You *could* make it more interesting. Join the book club, woo some hockey moms, do a *little* self-reinvention."

I deadpan. "Hard pass."

He just smirks. "Fine. But when you come back in a month *still* trying to prove you're not a reckless, commitment-phobic wildcard, don't say I didn't try to help."

I grunt and work on finishing my beer.

Michigan will be good for me.

No distractions. No PR nightmares. No bull.

Just me, the lake, and a much-needed break.

What could possibly go wrong?

3

UNWELCOME SUPRISES

Scarlett

The moment I step into the grocery store, I take a deep breath, inhaling the familiar scent of fresh produce, stale air conditioning, and a bakery section aggressively pushing day-old muffins. It's comforting, in a strange way. I've barely been here a day, but this already feels better. The lake breeze, the quiet, the absolute *lack* of people needing anything from me.

Glorious.

This summer is going to be exactly what I need. Just me, my laptop, a scenic view, and a desperate attempt to salvage my career before my editor sends a hitman to my house.

I grab a shopping cart and mentally run through my shopping list: coffee, fruit, snacks, and enough wine to drown my writer's block. Easy meals, because cooking is not my spiritual gift.

I head straight for the coffee aisle first. Because, priorities.

As I reach for a bag of dark roast, another hand moves at the exact same time, bumping against mine.

"Seriously?" I mutter, stepping back.

"Gotta say, wasn't expecting competition for coffee selection in the middle of a Tuesday afternoon," comes a deep, amused voice.

I turn, prepared to give my best *I'm just here for caffeine, not conversation* glare, and—okay. Wow.

The guy standing beside me is built like a linebacker, over six feet tall, with broad shoulders, messy dark hair, and an infuriating smirk that tells me he enjoys being irritating. He's got that whole *I could chop wood shirtless in a cologne commercial* vibe going for him, and I already hate that I noticed.

"Not competition," I say flatly, grabbing the coffee and tossing it into my basket. "Just someone trying to get in and out of this store as quickly as possible."

He arches a brow. "Not much for small talk, huh?"

I blink. "Are *you* the designated grocery store greeter? Because if so, I'd like to speak to management."

The smirk widens, like he's enjoying this.

Great. I've somehow stumbled across the *one* extrovert in this entire town.

"Sorry, sweetheart, no management here," he says, reaching for his own bag of coffee.

I ignore the *sweetheart* because, frankly, I don't have the time or the energy. I push my cart ahead and move to the next aisle—snacks. If I'm going to have any chance of survival this summer, I need fuel. Preferably in the form of carbs and salt.

Unfortunately, *he* seems to have the exact same shopping strategy.

"Following me now?" I ask, eyeing him as he grabs a bag of kettle chips from the same shelf I'm reaching for.

He laughs, leaning casually against his cart like he has all the time in the world. "Yeah, definitely tailing you for snack recommendations. What's next? Popcorn? Frozen pizzas?"

I narrow my eyes. "You are *so* unoriginal. You can't just repeat everything I pick."

"Can and will." He tosses a bag of pretzels into his cart with zero shame. "You seem like you know what you're doing."

I push ahead, stopping in front of a display and frown. "No oat milk," I mutter.

"I didn't know oats could make milk," Mr. Mind-Your-Own-Business says, coming up from behind me.

"Wow. *Amazing* flirting strategy." I move past

him, fully ready to leave *whoever this guy is* in my rearview mirror.

"You think I'm flirting?" He follows me again, clearly having way too much fun with this. "And here I thought we were just having a friendly chat."

I stop in my tracks, turning slowly. "I'm sorry, do I have a sign on my back that says '*I love small talk*'?"

He grins, like he's been waiting for this moment, but rather than answer, he just chuckles.

For some reason, I keep talking. Maybe it's the way he's looking at me, like he's surprised by my lack of interest. "I don't mean to be rude; I just came here for the summer to escape people."

At this, his eyebrows shoot up. "That might be difficult in a beachside tourist town." Then he extends a hand, as if this is some kind of *charming* introduction. "Chase."

I don't take it. Don't smile. "Scarlett."

His grin deepens, like he's pleased to finally have my name. "Scarlett. Huh. Nice to meet you. Maybe I'll see you around this summer."

I certainly hope not.

I let out a long, slow breath. *This is fine.* I am a mature, rational adult. I can handle an overly friendly fellow grocery store patron.

I spin on my heel and head for the frozen aisle, but apparently, we both need ice cream.

And there's only *one* carton of my favorite flavor left.

I reach for it at the exact same moment he does.

"Oh, come *on*," I exhale, exasperated.

He grins, fingers gripping the other side of the carton. "You again."

"*You* again." I tug the container toward me.

He tugs it back.

We stare each other down like two cowboys in an old Western standoff, a single pint of chocolate peanut butter swirl between us.

"Be reasonable," I say. "I had it first."

"Nope. I touched it first."

"That is a *lie.*"

He smirks. "Fine. You want to settle this like adults?"

I cross my arms. "I am not arm wrestling you in the middle of the frozen food aisle."

"Scared you'll lose?"

"Scared I'll break your fragile ego."

He lets out a low laugh, then—*the audacity*—grabs a second carton of some other flavor and holds it out to me. "Tell you what. You take this, and I take this one. A compromise."

I scowl at the offensive carton in his hand. "That's *mint chocolate chip.*"

"And?"

I look at him like he's personally insulted my entire family. "It tastes like frozen toothpaste."

"Well, now you're just being dramatic."

I yank the chocolate peanut butter swirl out of his hands and shove the mint back in the freezer. "Find another coping mechanism. This is mine."

I march toward the registers before he can argue.

Only to realize *he* has reached the checkout first.

With the last jar of peanut butter sitting smugly in his cart.

You have *got* to be kidding me.

I narrow my eyes at the cashier, a teenage girl who looks half-asleep but *also* looks like she might be susceptible to a small bribe.

I pull out a five-dollar bill and slide it across the counter. "You see that jar of peanut butter? If another shipment comes in, set one aside for me. Every week."

She perks up slightly, pocketing the cash. "Sure."

But then—

"Hey, Ashlyn," Chase says smoothly, leaning against the counter like he's the *star* of some rom-com meet-cute. "Got a question for you."

The cashier, Ashlyn, *giggles*. Actually *giggles*.

My stomach sinks.

"You wouldn't happen to have any more oat milk in the back, would you?" he asks, flashing a *dimple*.

Ashlyn perks up at Chase's question. "Actually, Mrs. Carter had one in her cart, but I think she left without buying it."

My stomach unclenches slightly. *Okay, so there's still one left. Good. I'll just—*

Chase turns toward the sweet old woman bagging her groceries nearby, flashes the kind of grin that probably got him out of detention as a kid, and says, "Mrs. Carter, right? You wouldn't happen to still have that oat milk, would you?"

She blinks up at him, then smiles, absolutely *charmed*. "Oh, yes, dear. Did you need it?"

"Wouldn't say *need*," he replies, voice smooth as butter. "But I sure would appreciate it. Haven't been able to find the stuff anywhere."

"Oh, in that case, take it," she says, handing it over with zero hesitation. "I was just going to try it, but I don't really need it."

Chase takes the oat milk with a *freaking* wink. "You're the best."

I *gape* as he drops it smugly into his cart, then looks at me like he just won an Olympic event.

I point an accusatory finger. "Yo*u scamm*ed an old lady."

"Sh*e offered* it to me," he says with a shrug.

Ashlyn, the *traitor*, giggles behind the register.

As soon as I've paid, I exhale sharply, grab my bags, and march toward the exit.

I *will not* let some overly confident, *annoyingly attractive* guy disrupt my peaceful summer.

This is my sanctuary. My escape.

And I am *not* here for distractions.

Even if they come with stupidly pretty blue eyes and a dimple that should honestly be illegal.

4

THE GIRL NEXT DOOR

Chase

The rental is perfect.

It's a charming two-story Craftsman with gray cedar shingles and crisp white trim, perched just high enough on the dunes to offer a stunning view of the lake. A wraparound porch, complete with a couple of wooden rocking chairs, faces the water, and there's a private path that leads straight to the beach.

Inside, the space is designed for easy living—vaulted ceilings, large windows, and hardwood floors worn soft by sand-dusted feet. The kitchen is small but functional, and the living room features an overstuffed couch that looks as if it was made for post-beach naps.

I drop my grocery bags onto the counter and take it all in.

This is exactly what I need.

No packed schedules, no pressure from the front office, no cameras in my face. Just me, my dog, and an entire summer to clear my head before my contract negotiations ramp up.

I slide a few items into the fridge, then pause when I realize Rip isn't glued to my side anymore.

"Rip?"

Silence.

Shit.

I glance toward the sliding glass doors that lead to the back deck, and sure enough, they're cracked open just enough for an 80-pound mass of pure disobedience to squeeze through.

I walk outside and scan the dunes until I spot him.

In *her* yard.

The woman from the grocery store.

She doesn't see me yet. She's crouched in the grass, her long fingers scratching behind Rip's ears while my traitorous dog soaks it up like she's the best thing that's ever happened to him.

"You're such a *good* boy," she coos, her voice softer than I've heard it.

Rip is loving it. He has a big, dumb, tongue-lolling grin, his paws planted firmly on her thighs, as if he's already chosen her as his new favorite person.

My damn dog.

I take a moment to size her up in the daylight.

She's tall—maybe five-eight or five-nine. Long legs, toned but soft in all the right places, tanned like she's spent some time in the sun. Her dark brown hair is flecked with gold and blows gently in the breeze.

And her face?

Would be gorgeous—if she didn't look like the type of woman who could destroy a man for sport. High cheekbones, full lips, and expressive brown eyes that seem to assess everything and everyone with instant judgment. A perfect little nose that wrinkles slightly when she's amused—and from what I can tell, she's not amused by me *at all*.

She looks like she'd be *devastating* if she smiled at a guy.

Not that I'll ever be on the receiving end of it.

I clear my throat and step off my deck and into the grass.

She lifts her head, and just like that, her entire demeanor shifts.

Her expression closes off. Her fingers stop scratching behind Rip's ears. The warmth in her face vanishes so quickly it's almost impressive.

"Well, well, well," I drawl, crossing my arms as I approach. "You sure change your tune when you don't realize you're talking to *my* dog."

Her lips press together as she straightens.

"I wasn't talking to *you*," she replies coolly.

"No, but I still feel personally betrayed." I glance at Rip, who is sitting obediently at her feet, tail thumping the grass like she's his long-lost soulmate. "*Seriously?*"

She lifts a single brow. "Maybe he has good taste."

I scoff.

She exhales, turning back to Rip. "Go home, buddy."

Rip does not go home. Rip leans harder against her legs, as if sensing the chance to ruin my life.

I huff and step forward, slapping my thigh. "Rip, let's go."

Nothing.

She lifts her chin, looking smug. "Looks like he's made his choice."

"You feeding him steak over here or something?"

"Just some affection." She scratches him one last time, then sighs. "I *guess* you can stay."

I frown. "Were you talking to *me* or the dog?"

She gives me a once-over. "Not entirely sure yet."

I arch a brow. "You always this charming?"

"Only for people who deserve it."

Jeez, she's *mean*.

And—annoyingly—kind of hot when she is.

I kneel, giving Rip a quick chin scratch. "You really gonna abandon me for some woman you just met?"

Rip sneezes.

Scottie smirks. "Guess that's a yes."

I exhale sharply, straightening. "Look, as much as I'm loving our *continued* run-ins, I need my dog back."

She shrugs. "That's between you and him."

I reach into my back pocket, pull out a dog treat, and hold it up. "Rip. Come."

Rip *finally* moves, trotting over as if I didn't just watch him abandon our entire relationship for some stranger with a nice voice.

She watches, unimpressed. "Weak."

I shoot her a look as I snap Rip's collar. "So, what's your story? Just renting this place for the weekend?"

She groans. "Same for you, I guess?"

"Nope." I grin. "I'm here all month."

She closes her eyes briefly, like she's *physically* restraining herself from committing a crime. "Great. That's great."

I chuckle. "What about you?"

She exhales. "Yeah. Here for a month. I need peace and quiet. I'm working."

"Working?"

She sighs, as if dreading the conversation. "My next book is overdue to my publisher."

I'm suddenly curious. "What do you write?"

She hesitates, then finally mutters, "Nonfiction."

Nonfiction. *Okay.*

She's being cagey as hell about it, though, so I press. "Like what?"

She lets out a slow breath, staring at the ground for a moment before finally looking up. "My first book was called *The Love Delusion: Why Romance is the Greatest Scam in Human History.*"

I blink.

And then it clicks.

I *know* that title.

I tilt my head, staring at her. "Wait. You're *Scottie Calloway?*"

She sighs, like she already knows where this is going.

I grin. *Oh, this is too good.*

"You're, like, a big deal."

"Don't," she says flatly.

"No, no, I mean—wow." I laugh, shaking my head. "My teammate's girlfriend is obsessed with your books."

She blinks, confused.

I wave a hand. "Doesn't matter. What *does* matter is that I now understand *exactly* why you're such a delight."

She crosses her arms, unimpressed. "And what's that supposed to mean?"

I smirk. "Nothing." I was right—she's a total man-eater.

Her nostrils flare slightly.

The best part about this situation? She obviously has no clue who *I* am.

I lean a shoulder against the porch railing, crossing my arms. "You really don't know who I am, do you?"

Her brows pull together slightly. "Am I supposed to?"

I blink. "I play for the Dallas Stampede."

She gives me a blank look.

I resist the urge to run a hand down my face. "The hockey team."

A slow nod, as if she's trying to place the name.

"The sport with sticks and pucks...played on ice..."

That earns me an eye roll. "I *know* what hockey is."

"Didn't seem like it."

"I'm from Dallas; I just...don't watch hockey."

"Really? You're from Dallas?"

She nods.

That's random.

"And you don't watch hockey *at all?*" I let out a low whistle. "Damn."

"Sorry to bruise your ego," she says, not sounding sorry at all.

"I'll live."

She shifts slightly, arms still crossed, her gaze darting toward my house—how close it is to her place. A mere thirty feet away.

"I guess I'll see you around," I say.

Her hands go to her hips as I retreat toward my porch, still smirking. "I need peace and quiet, so try to keep it down," she calls after me.

I let out a low chuckle as I push inside, Rip trotting in behind me.

I have no idea what just happened out there, but damn—this summer *just* got more fun.

The sun is setting by the time I step outside, Rip at my heels, still looking smug about his earlier betrayal. I run a hand through his fur absentmindedly, my gaze flicking toward Scarlett's house. Her porch light is on, casting a warm glow over the front steps.

I stare at the carton of oat milk in my hand for a moment, debating.

I could keep it. It's not like I *need* it, but keeping it out of spite would be a little *too* petty, even for me. And maybe—just maybe—I don't totally hate the idea of throwing her off her game.

So, before I can overthink it, I walk over, place the carton neatly by her front door, and turn back before I do something stupid. Like knock. Or stick around to see her reaction.

I'm halfway up my own porch steps when Rip

lets out a low huff, looking back toward her house.

"Don't give me that look," I mutter, pushing my door open. "I *can* be nice."

Not that I plan on making it a habit.

The smell of charcoal and sizzling burgers hangs thick in the warm Michigan air as I step onto my parents' back deck. The yard looks the same as it always has—worn Adirondack chairs circled around a fire pit, the wooden fence still half-painted from the summer Dad got ambitious and then promptly gave up. There's a cooler of drinks by the grill, and the sound of laughter filters through the screen door as Evie argues with Owen about something that probably doesn't matter.

It's good to be home. Familiar.

"About time," my dad grumbles, flipping a burger. "We were starting to think you got lost."

"I almost *did* get lost." I set down a six-pack of beer and smirk. It's probably a sign that it's been too long since I've been home—or that the town has changed since I lived here a dozen years ago.

Mom shakes her head at me, but her smile softens her expression. "Sit. Eat. Tell us about your life, since your sister says you've been avoiding actual conversation."

Evie rolls her eyes. "Because he *has*."

I grab a plate and drop into one of the chairs. "Not avoiding. Just busy."

Dad snorts. "Busy doing what? It's the off-season."

"Training," I lie smoothly, taking a sip of my drink. "Getting my mind right before next year."

They all exchange a look, the one that says *we weren't born yesterday, Chase.*

I don't want them to worry. They have enough on their plates without me adding my uncertain future to the pile.

Owen shifts in his chair, adjusting his position in his wheelchair. "You still thinking about that captaincy thing?" he asks.

I glance at him. Owen doesn't ask questions unless he really wants to know. He's never been one for small talk, not since the accident. For a second, I consider telling him everything—how the team's been hinting that I need to clean up my image, how the contract renewal feels like a weight I can't shake, how I'm starting to wonder if I'm really cut out for it at all.

But instead, I just shrug. "Something like that."

Owen studies me for a beat before nodding. "You'd be good at it."

My chest tightens, and I clear my throat. "Yeah, well. We'll see."

Mom, ever perceptive, cuts in before the conversation can get heavier. "Tell us about this neighbor of yours," she says, throwing me a knowing look. "Evie mentioned something about a *famous* writer?"

I groan. "Not this again." I should never have texted my twin sister about that.

Evie smirks. "So, I Googled her, and she's really pretty too."

I sigh, ignoring that remark, and lean back in my chair. "She's a bestselling author, yeah. But she's also the most infuriating human being I've ever met. Hates my guts for *no reason*."

Dad arches a brow. "No reason at all?"

"None."

Owen chuckles. "I bet she has a reason."

I scowl. "Well, *I* don't know what it is."

Mom hums, flipping the burgers on the grill. "Are you sure she actually hates you?"

"Uh, yeah. The woman practically set me on fire with a look, and we've spoken all of twice."

Evie snickers. "She wouldn't be the first."

I ignore her. "She's just *angry*. It's exhausting."

Mom turns, wiping her hands on a dish towel. "People who walk around with that much anger usually aren't really mad at *you*, honey. They're mad at something else. You just happen to be in the line of fire."

That makes me pause.

Because, yeah, Scarlett *is* angry. And I've done nothing. I've met plenty of people who don't like me, but this is different.

She has a wall up so thick it's practically made of reinforced steel.

For some reason, I can't help wanting to break through.

Owen smirks. "Sounds like you like her."

"Absolutely not," I say quickly.

Evie grins. "I don't know, Chase. You seem pretty interested."

I groan, dragging a hand down my face. "You all suck."

Mom pats my shoulder, smiling in that way only moms can. "Just be nice, sweetheart."

"Don't tell me you're *siding* with her."

Mom winks. "I'm just saying… sometimes the people who frustrate us the most are the ones we end up learning the most from."

I shake my head, but something about that settles deep in my chest. I sip my IPA and wonder if Mom's right. If Scarlett's not actually mad at *me*, what's she so angry about?

5

MY (UN)HAPPY PLACE

Scarlett

I stroll through the quaint town, past a coffee shop and a small café, my phone pressed to my ear, window shopping as I listen to Harper's voice on the other end of the line.

"Well... how's Michigan?" she asks.

"Fine so far. The house is great. There's a hockey player living next door."

A pause. "Is he famous?"

"I don't know."

"What's his name?"

"Chase something," I grumble, recalling the man who tried to steal my peanut butter swirl. "He plays for Dallas."

"Please hold," Harper says, and I hear her clicking on her keyboard. She's practically attached to her laptop. "Oh, what do we have here?" She makes a breathy sound. "He just *looks* like a good time."

I growl. "Can you not!?"

"Fine… how's the writing going?" she asks, amusement lacing her tone.

I sigh, tilting my head back to soak in the sun. "Well, let's see… I've successfully consumed an entire family-sized bag of pretzels, started and abandoned three different playlists for inspiration, and stared at a blinking cursor long enough to be declared legally insane."

"So… not great?"

"Not great," I confirm.

Harper hums, ever patient. "Scottie, it's a process. The reclaiming of your creative self doesn't happen overnight. You're not a vending machine where you press a button and get a book. Give yourself time."

I exhale, rubbing my temple. "I don't *have* time, Harp. I have a deadline."

"What you have," she corrects, "is a brain that's been running on empty. Give it a minute, girl. Sit in the sun. Put your toes in the water. Have a cocktail. The words will come."

Maybe she's right; it has only been three days.

I drag my gaze to the gentle waves rolling against the shore a few blocks away, the Lake Michigan breeze carrying the scent of fresh water and sand. It *is* peaceful here. And it's been… nice. *Mostly*. Thankfully, I haven't had any more run-ins with my irritating next-door neighbor. I did see his cute dog yesterday morning napping on the deck.

"Maybe you're right," I admit, strolling past an old-fashioned candy shoppe I'll definitely circle back to later. "I'll work on the relaxing thing."

"Good. And if that fails, try doing something that makes you *not* think about the book. Go for a walk. Read something fun. Flirt with a cute hockey player. Just *be* for a little while."

"Harper, I can't just—"

"Yes, you can," she interrupts. "Trust me. Do something that reminds you why you love stories in the first place."

I sigh, adjusting my bag over my shoulder. "Fine. But I gotta go. I'm in town running errands."

"Just promise me you won't stress yourself into an early grave, okay?"

"I make no promises."

She snorts. "Have a cocktail, Calloway."

I roll my eyes and hang up, slipping my phone into my pocket as I step inside the town's small bookstore.

The place is straight out of a Hallmark movie— soft amber lighting, wooden shelves packed with books, a tiny café in the corner where a barista in a vintage apron is frothing milk for a latte. The scent of coffee and paper surrounds me, and despite my best efforts, a small part of me *does* feel a little lighter stepping inside.

Harper's words float through my head again.

Something that reminds you why you love stories in the first place.

I trail my fingers along the spines of the books on the nearest table, allowing myself to just *be* for a moment. I enjoy their colorful covers and vibrant designs…

And then I hear it.

A deep, familiar voice.

I freeze, my pulse kicking up.

No.

No, no, no.

I subtly step behind a nearby display of newly released paperbacks, peeking between the stacks.

And there he is.

All six foot three inches of Chase Remington. (Yes, I'd Googled him—apparently, he's a pretty big deal if you're into hockey, which I definitely am *not*.)

He's in jeans and a T-shirt, looking obnoxiously relaxed as he scans the shelves like he has *any* business being in a bookstore.

What are the odds?

I press my back against the display and exhale sharply. I could be civilized; I could thank him for the oat milk, but I *won't*. Because it should have been mine on *principle*.

I take a slow step backward, contemplating my escape. If I can just make it to the door—

"Scarlett."

Crap.

I close my eyes, steeling myself before turning to face him. He's leaning against a bookshelf, arms crossed, looking far too pleased with himself.

"You *again*?" I say, exasperated.

He lifts a brow. "You hiding from me?"

I scoff. "You wish."

His mouth twitches like he's holding back a smirk, but before he can respond, a flirty-looking store clerk approaches with a bright, eager smile.

"Can I help you two find anything?" she asks.

Gross. Her assumption that we're here together is atrocious.

I open my mouth to say *no,* but Chase beats me to it.

"Actually, yeah." He turns to her, all lazy charm. "Do you have a romance section?"

The clerk's eyes light up. "Yes! We have an entire section, *and* we carry all the books from the Stampede's romance book club!"

My stomach *plummets.*

Chase grins, his gaze sliding back to mine. "Cool, huh?"

I groan, fighting the urge to hurl a hardcover at his head. "You have *got* to be kidding me."

During my Googling, I'd seen some nonsense about how the team was sponsoring a book club. As if the guys sit around in the locker room reading rom-coms. Gag me with a wooden spoon.

He smirks, clearly entertained by my distress. "What? I just figured I could grab myself a beach read, maybe see what all the hype is about."

I narrow my eyes. "You don't read romance."

He gives me a pointed look; it's a look that says he knows something I don't, and I feel it deep inside my stomach. *Weird.* "How would you know?" he asks, amusement lacing his voice.

"Because." I wave a hand at him. "You're *you*."

His smirk deepens. "Maybe I'm just looking for something *empowering*. You know, about how women don't need men."

My jaw locks. "You're such a pain in the—"

"Right this way!" the clerk chirps, oblivious to the tension.

I sigh. This is *not* how I imagined my peaceful afternoon going.

A bookstore is supposed to be *my* territory, *my* happy place. He just managed to ruin that in about four seconds.

And yet, somehow, I find myself following Chase straight into the depths of my own personal hell.

6

NEW TERRITORY

Chase

Scarlett follows the bookstore clerk reluctantly, and I trail behind, enjoying the show. She's clearly on edge, trying so hard not to let me get under her skin. It's adorable, really.

"Here we are," the clerk chirps, gesturing toward a shelf with a flourish. It's labeled Non-Fiction, filled with heavy, serious-looking titles—dark covers and blocky lettering. Supposedly, this is where her books live. It's not surprising that she writes such serious material; her personality isn't exactly warm and fuzzy.

The clerk searches, running a finger along the spines. "Huh."

Scarlett's eyes scan the display, her brows furrowing.

"Huh?" I echo, rocking back on my heels.

She frowns, shifting her stance and scanning higher, then lower. I fight the urge to smirk.

"Everything okay?" I ask, feigning innocence.

Scarlett shoots me a look that says she'd rather eat glass than admit whatever's bothering her, but the tension rolling off her gives her away.

The clerk finally locates the book in question. "Oh, here it is!" she says brightly, crouching down and pulling it from the very bottom shelf, where it was buried between two thicker volumes.

I glance between Scarlett and the sad, dust-covered book. I don't have to say a damn thing; her expression is already murderous.

She crosses her arms. "Wow. What a place of honor."

I bite my lip to keep from laughing. "Tough break, Calloway."

She ignores me, taking the book from the clerk and flipping through it, muttering under her breath about *algorithm biases and mainstream book club pandering*.

I lean casually against a nearby shelf, giving her a once-over.

I wasn't wrong before—she is hot. I mean, she's been hot since the second I laid eyes on her. But today? With her sun-kissed skin and hair that looks like she just rolled out of bed in the best way possible? It's unfair, really. Cut-off jean shorts, tan sandals, and a white cotton sweater. She looks like she belongs in Nantucket.

"You look like you got some sun, Calloway," I remark casually.

She eyes me warily. "Yeah? And what does that mean, exactly?"

I tilt my head, studying her. "Just that the lake's treating you well. A little sun-kissed glow. Healthy. Radiant."

She rolls her eyes. "Flattery won't work on me, Remington."

I grin, slow and lazy. "Using my last name... which I never gave you. Someone looked me up." She turns six shades of red. *Interesting*.

"Well, in case you're wondering, I did not come here for a tan. I came here to work."

I lift a brow. "Sure. That's why you've been frolicking around in the sun like you're in a Nicholas Sparks movie."

Scarlett glares. "I was reading on the deck."

"Reading *what* exactly? A steamy romance? Taking notes?"

Her lips press together, and I can *see* the effort it takes her not to throw the book in her hands directly at my face.

"Not all of us spend our free time indulging in unrealistic fantasies, *Remington*."

And since I lack self-control, I lean in just a fraction, dropping my voice. "Shame. Maybe you could use a good fantasy or two."

Scarlett's breath catches for just a second—a flicker of something—anger? Yep, definitely anger.

My mom's words replay in my head—*they're mad at something else. You just happen to be in the line of fire.*

"Oh! We just got a new shipment of the Stampede book club picks," the clerk says cheerfully, oblivious to the storm brewing between us. "Want me to show you?"

I really had no idea she was still standing here.

Scarlett looks about ready to bolt, so obviously, I don't give her the option.

"Actually, yeah," I say, flashing the clerk a grin. "Maybe they've got a good enemies-to-lovers rec?"

Scarlett huffs a quiet noise of disbelief beside me. I hear it. I feel it.

"I figured you'd appreciate the genre," I add, shooting her a knowing glance. "Since, you know, we're living it."

Her nails dig into her book. "We are not living anything."

"Sure," I say easily, grinning. "Tell yourself that."

She sucks in a breath like she's about to unleash hell on me, but then the clerk pipes up, holding a romance novel in each hand. "Ooh, we've got a few classics! Would you rather something with a slow burn or more of a forced proximity angle?"

Scarlett looks horrified. I swear I hear her soul trying to leave her body.

"I think we're good," she says quickly, shaking her head.

"Actually," I interrupt, stepping over to the register, "I think I found what I came for." I lift the dust-covered book in my hand and head for the checkout counter.

Scarlett blinks at it. Then at me. "You—"

"Buying your book?" I finish for her, flashing a grin. "Yeah."

Her eyes narrow. "Why?"

I shrug, pulling out my wallet. "What can I say? It speaks to me."

I finally glance down at the title.

How to Die Alone (and Love Every Second of It).

I grin. "Dark. I love it."

Scarlett crosses her arms, her nostrils flaring, which, of course, makes me even more smug.

I whistle as I slide the book toward the clerk, grab a random bookmark, and run my black AmEx card through the card reader.

Then, without another word, I turn and stroll toward the door.

I don't need to look back to know she's still standing there, looking utterly aghast.

7

MAKE IT MAKE SENSE

Chase

A small Korean woman is sitting on a beach towel in front of Scarlett's house.

Huh.

Did she check out early? A pang of disappointment courses through me before I can stop it.

"Scottie!" the woman calls over one shoulder. "Bring me another marg when you come out!"

Okay, so she's definitely not checked out. She's very much still here.

Then Scarlett steps out onto the deck, and my brain completely malfunctions.

I'm talking full system failure.

Because she's in a bathing suit.

Not the modest, hide-your-assets kind either. Nope. It's one of those sleek, high-cut numbers that's somehow even hotter than if she were wearing barely anything at all. Her legs look endless, and the way the material clings to her curves makes my mouth go dry.

Scarlett Calloway in a bikini is something I absolutely was not prepared for today.

I turn back toward the water, gripping the tennis ball in my hand with more force than necessary before launching it for Rip, who sprints into the surf like his life depends on it.

Evie, stretched out beside me on a towel, watches with an obnoxiously knowing smirk.

"What?" I grumble.

"Oh, nothing," she replies, flipping a page in her book. "Just enjoying the show."

I glance over at her. "What show?"

Evie doesn't even look up. "The one where you pretend you're not interested in your neighbor while your eyeballs nearly fall out of your head just now."

I scowl, tossing the ball for Rip again. "I was caught off guard."

"Uh-huh."

"She's infuriating."

"Sure."

"I'd rather let a Zamboni run over my foot than deal with her for the rest of the summer."

Evie finally looks up from her book, eyebrows raised. "And yet, you keep staring."

I don't dignify that with a response.

Instead, I focus on the fact that Scarlett is making her way down to the beach—*with a tray of margaritas*.

This day just keeps getting more interesting. It's two o'clock in the afternoon, and they're drinking tequila. I like where this is going.

The woman on the towel hops up, sunglasses pushed to the top of her head. "That was *so* slow. I'm dying of thirst."

Scarlett shoves the tray at her. "You're dramatic."

Her friend lifts one of the glasses, clinking the ice cubes. "And you're grumpy, but I still love you."

They exchange a look before both taking a sip, and yeah, okay—I'm intrigued.

Evie's smirk deepens as she watches them. "You should introduce me."

I sigh and shake my head, but before I can say anything, Rip comes barreling out of the water, shaking spray everywhere.

"Ugh, buddy, *really*?" Evie says, giving him a glare.

Rip ignores Evie and trots over to greet his new favorite person.

"Oh my gosh," Scarlett's friend gasps, immediately crouching down and scratching behind Rip's ears like they've known each other for years. "This is the most beautiful dog I've ever seen."

Rip, the traitorous bastard, eats it up, shoving his entire weight against her and closing his eyes in bliss.

"I'm *Harper*," she says, still scratching Rip. "And who are you, handsome boy?"

"That's Rip," I reply, wandering over. I nod toward Scarlett and her companion. "He has excellent taste."

"Doubtful," she mutters, but I catch the way her lips twitch as she fights a smile.

Harper straightens, still rubbing Rip's ears. "I'm Harper."

"Chase," I say, nodding toward Scarlett. "You must be the one she's been venting to about me."

Harper grins. "Oh, *nonstop*."

Scarlett hisses, "Harper!"

"What?" She shrugs. "I'm just making conversation."

I smirk.

Scarlett rolls her eyes. "Believe it or not, *Remington*, my life doesn't revolve around you."

"But apparently, it does include regular discussions about me," I tease.

Evie strolls over to where I'm standing.

Harper fake-whispers to Evie, "This is the best thing I've ever seen."

Evie hums in agreement. "I'm fully invested."

Scarlett glares at both of them.

I toss the ball for Rip again and turn to my sister. "Anyway, this is Evie, my twin sister."

"Scarlett's best friend," Harper says with a knowing look. "Chase's twin sister. Yeah, I feel like we're gonna get along just fine."

Evie grins. "I already like you."

Scarlett takes a long sip of her drink, then levels her gaze at me. "So *that's* why you're so annoying. You were born with double the amount of cockiness a normal person should have."

Evie laughs. "Oh, I *really* like her."

Scarlett turns to her. "That wasn't a compliment."

"Well, I took it as one anyway."

Harper claps her hands together. "Okay, so this is fun."

"For *you*," Scarlett grumbles, looking ready to bolt.

"Oh, come on, Scottie. Stay," Harper says, patting the towel next to her.

Scarlett, or as everyone else calls her, Scottie, levels her friend with a glare that could topple a building.

I smirk. "Yeah, Scottie. Stay."

Scarlett's gaze snaps to mine, fire blazing in her eyes. *Do not look at her chest. Do not look at her chest.*

Then—much to everyone's shock, including my own—Scarlett *sits.*

Right there, on the towel, her lips pursed as if

she already regrets it.

I raise an eyebrow. "Wow. I thought you'd put up more of a fight."

She grabs a handful of sand and *chucks* it at me.

Harper and my sister absolutely *die* laughing.

Rip? He trots up and lays down between us, tail wagging, blissfully oblivious to the war that's just been declared.

Scarlett is still glaring at me when Rip decides he's had enough lounging and sprints back toward the water. I push up from the sand and follow, bracing myself before heading into the waves. The water is perfectly cold—refreshing without being unbearable—and I waste no time diving under, resurfacing with a shake of my hair.

When I glance back toward the shore, I expect to see Scarlett firmly planted in her dry, safe space, arms crossed, drink in hand.

Instead, she's... wading in?

I pause, watching as she steps into the surf, clearly debating her life choices. Harper calls something to her from the sand, but Scarlett just flips her off and keeps going.

Huh. *Color me impressed.*

I don't know why I assumed she'd be the type to stay firmly on dry land, but there's something captivating about seeing her here, sunlight glinting off her damp skin, waves lapping at her legs as she cautiously ventures deeper.

She doesn't hesitate in her convictions, but when it comes to the actual water? She's clearly second-guessing.

It's kind of cute.

I'm about to comment on it—because obviously, I have to—when a particularly strong wave rushes in out of nowhere.

It slams into Scarlett's back like it has a personal vendetta against her, and before she can brace herself—

"Oh, *shit*—"

She disappears.

I blink.

One second, she's standing there; the next, she's gone, swallowed by the waves.

"Scarlett?" I call, taking a few steps closer.

Nothing.

Rip barks excitedly, as if this is the best game ever, his tail wagging as he paddles past me.

Then—Scarlett reemerges, sputtering, hair plastered to her face, arms flailing.

I lose it.

I actually have to bend at the waist, hands on my knees, because I'm laughing so hard.

Scarlett, however, does *not* find it funny.

She gasps, shoving her wet hair out of her face, struggling against the pull of the water as she tries to regain her footing. *"What the hell was that?!"*

"Uh, a wave?" I manage between laughs.

"*A rogue* tsunami," she mutters, finally righting herself—only to immediately *screech* and start flailing again.

My laughter doubles. "Now what?"

"Something touched me!"

Oh, this just keeps getting better.

I wade over, thoroughly entertained. "You okay?"

She *glares* at me. "I swear to you, something grabbed my leg."

Then she *screams* again, lunging forward and latching onto my shoulders like I'm some kind of human flotation device.

I barely have time to react before she's *climbing me like a* tree, her legs wrapping around my waist, her hands clutching my shoulders in a death grip. Her skin is slick with lake water, sliding against mine as she tries to get higher, away from whatever she thinks is after her. Every shift presses her closer, her thighs gripping my hips, her chest flush against mine.

I blink down at her, her face pressed against my neck.

Well.

This took an *unexpected* turn.

"Uh…" I clear my throat. "Not that I'm complaining, but usually when a woman throws herself at me, it's under much different circumstances."

She smacks my shoulder. *"This is not* funny!"

"It's a *little* funny."

She pulls back just enough to glare at me, her dark eyes furious and—damn it—annoyingly gorgeous up close. Water droplets cling to her lashes, and I can feel her breath against my mouth, warm compared to the cool lake air. Her fingers dig into my shoulders, nails leaving little crescents I'll probably feel tomorrow.

"I will *end* you, Remington."

I smirk. "Bold words for someone literally clinging to me for dear life."

She shudders, tightening her hold. "I *felt* something. I swear, if it was a jellyfish—"

I shift my grip on her, steadying her in my arms because, honestly? She's not *that* heavy, and I'm kind of enjoying this. My hands find purchase on the backs of her thighs, her skin cool and smooth beneath my palms. Every time she shudders, I feel it everywhere—the tremor running through her body into mine.

"More likely seaweed."

She gasps, shoving at my chest. *"Get it off me!"*

I hold back another laugh. "I can't see it if you don't let me put you down."

"Nope. Not happening."

"So you're just going to live up here now?"

"Maybe."

I snort. "It's seaweed, not the Loch Ness monster. But if you're scared, I guess I could carry you back to shore—"

"*I'm not* scared.*"

"You sure about that?"

That's when I realize this position—her wrapped around me, wet and warm, pressing closer with every wave—is about to become a problem. My body starts to tighten in ways that have absolutely no business in a water rescue.

Do not go there, Remington. You're a grown man, not a thirteen-year-old who just discovered the Victoria's Secret catalog. Focus on... seaweed. Very unsexy seaweed.

"Put me down."

"Say please."

"Don't make me kill you today, Remington."

I chuckle, finally letting her slide down. It's torture—the slow drag of her body against mine, wet skin on wet skin, her curves pressing into me the whole way down. My hands settle on her waist for a beat longer than necessary, thumbs brushing the strip of bare skin just above her bikini bottoms. She feels good pressed against me, warm and soft despite the cold water, her pulse fluttering under my fingertips.

The second her feet hit the sandbar, she shoves away from me, muttering something under her breath that sounds vaguely like *"arrogant* bastard."

I grin.

She insults me, and I smile.

Make it make sense.

She storms out of the water like an avenging sea goddess, shoulders tense, hair dripping, her hips swaying in a way that makes my mouth water.

Harper and Evie are waiting on shore, both of them openly wheezing with laughter.

Harper gasps. "That was *so* worth the trip."

Rip trots happily beside her, tail wagging, and immediately betrays me by rubbing his wet, sandy body all over Scarlett's legs.

I *lose it* again.

Scarlett looks to the sky as if she's questioning every life decision that led her to this moment.

Harper, still grinning, passes her a margarita. "Here. You *really* need this."

Scarlett takes a long sip and lets out a sigh of contentment.

I toss Rip's ball and shake my head, unable to wipe the smirk off my face.

This *summer* just keeps getting better.

After Scarlett downs half the margarita, I watch her settle back onto the towel, still muttering about "vicious seaweed attacks."

The other girls drift into their own conversations, and for a moment, it's just us—well, us and Rip, who has decided that Scarlett's leg makes an excellent pillow.

"You good?" I ask, dropping onto the sand next to her.

She's quiet for a beat, absently running her fingers through Rip's fur.

"I haven't been in the water in years."

"What, the Dallas pools don't do it for you?"

She shakes her head, a wry smile tugging at her lips. "Chlorine and screaming kids aren't quite the same as this." She gestures at the lake. "I forgot how... big it feels."

"Yeah?"

"The only water I deal with in Dallas is my bathtub," she says dryly.

Great. Now I'm thinking about Scarlett in a bathtub. I need to focus on literally anything else right now: hockey stats, golf scores, my grandmother's potato salad—anything.

I force my attention back to her face, where it's marginally safer.

She takes another sip of her drink. "Out here, you can't control anything. Waves come when they want. Seaweed attacks at will."

"Truly savage," I agree, fighting a grin.

She shoots me a look but continues. "I used to be good at this. The whole... letting go thing."

"What changed?"

She shrugs. "I guess I got better at holding on."

The admission is small, but something about the way she says it—like she's not sure if that's a good thing or not—makes me pay attention.

"Maybe you just need practice," I offer. "Start

small. Like not death-gripping the beach towel."

She looks down at her hands, which are indeed clutching the towel edges, and laughs. "Baby steps?"

"Exactly. Today seaweed, tomorrow... who knows what you'll be capable of."

"Let's not get crazy," she says, but she's smiling now, and her grip on the towel loosens.

"For what it's worth," I say, "you looked pretty invincible out there. Even with the seaweed vendetta."

She huffs a laugh, and some of the tension eases from her shoulders. "I looked like a deranged sea creature."

"A very attractive deranged sea creature."

This time, her laugh is genuine as she tips her head back, exposing the graceful curve of her throat. I struggle to keep my eyes off the droplets of water still clinging to her skin. "Your compliments need work, Remington."

Harper begins to ask about dinner plans, interrupting the moment. But as Scarlett stands up, brushing sand off her legs, she pauses. "Thanks," she says quietly. "For not making it weird."

"Anytime, Calloway."

8

DRINKS, DRAMA, AND A DANGEROUS AMOUNT OF EYE CONTACT

Scarlett

The shower helps—not just to rinse the lake off my skin, but to give me a solid five minutes of peace—five whole minutes without Chase Remington's smug face flashing in my brain. Five minutes where I don't have to think about how his hands felt on my waist when he "saved" me from a vicious seaweed attack or how irritatingly strong and steady he was, like he actually enjoyed swooping in to rescue me.

I wrap myself in a towel and step into the bedroom, where Harper is sprawled on my bed, flipping through a magazine as if she lives here.

"Tell me why we're going back over there again?" I ask, toweling off my hair.

Harper smirks, flipping a page. "Because they invited us."

"I don't recall agreeing."

"You did, actually. You nodded, which, in most cultures, counts as a yes."

I glare at her. "I was recovering from a near-death experience."

Harper rolls onto her side, grinning. "It was one tiny piece of seaweed."

I yank open my dresser drawer. "Well, it was traumatic."

She grins, unbothered by my foul mood. "I don't see what the problem is. Chase is hot, his sister is awesome, and there's free food. It's a win-win."

"The problem is that I came here to relax and work, not to socialize with professional hockey players and their cool, friendly siblings."

Harper levels me with a look. "Oh, yes. Because God forbid you enjoy yourself."

I throw a shirt at her head.

She laughs, batting it away, then watches as I dig through my limited wardrobe. "Please wear something cute," she says, feigning exhaustion. "You're in this perpetual state of man-repellent fashion, and I feel like, just once, I deserve to see you look a little flirty."

I raise a brow. "I am not dressing up for Chase."

Harper smirks. "I never said you were."

I grab the first thing I see—a pair of cutoffs and a soft navy tank top—and pull them on. "How's this?"

Harper studies me, then shrugs. "Eh. It'll do."

I roll my eyes. "Glad I have your approval."

Fifteen minutes later, we're making our way over to Chase's rental. The deck is lit with warm string lights, and the smell of grilling meat drifts toward us in the salty summer air. Rip is lounging at the base of the stairs like he owns the place, his big head lifting the second he spots me.

"Look at that," Harper muses. "Your only true friend on this trip."

I scratch behind Rip's ears, and the traitor rolls onto his back immediately, asking for belly rubs.

"You're embarrassing yourself," I murmur, rubbing his stomach anyway.

"Don't let Chase hear you talking sweet like that," Harper warns. "Wouldn't want him to know you're capable of affection."

I shoot her a glare, but before I can respond, Evie appears at the top of the stairs, waving us up. "Hey! Glad you came."

Harper bounds forward, all charm and easy conversation. "Wouldn't miss it."

I follow a little more slowly, steeling myself for whatever fresh hell Chase has in store for me.

He's standing at the grill, beer in hand, wearing a fitted T-shirt that clings to his torso in ways I'd rather not analyze.

His eyes flick to me, and that slow, insufferable grin spreads across his face. "Well, well. Look who survived the treacherous seaweed attack of 2025."

I ignore him and turn to Evie instead. "Thanks for having us."

She grins. "You're welcome anytime."

Chase makes a noise of protest, and I level him with a glare. "Do you have a problem?"

"Nope," he says easily, flipping a perfectly grilled steak kabob. "Just mentally preparing for the lecture you're going to give me about how meat is bad for my heart or whatever."

I grab a beer from the cooler. "I'm not a vegetarian."

Chase blinks. "You're not?"

"Why do you sound so shocked?"

"Because you're all…" He gestures vaguely at me. "You know. Misanthropic."

Harper snorts into her drink.

Evie elbows her brother. "You're an idiot."

He shrugs. "It's been said before."

Dinner is surprisingly… enjoyable. The kabobs are amazing. Evie and Harper talk about everything from travel to books to the most embarrassing things Chase has ever done (a list Evie provides with ruthless enthusiasm).

"Scottie's a bestselling author," Harper announces at one point, clearly proud. "She writes non-fiction—super empowering, smart, feminist stuff."

Evie lights up. "That's amazing! I need to read your books. What's your most recent one about?"

I pause, choosing my words carefully. "It's… about prioritizing yourself. About choosing happiness on your own terms instead of chasing relationships that don't serve you."

Chase smirks. "So, a fun, lighthearted beach read."

I glare at him.

Evie, however, looks thoughtful. "So, like, do you think everyone is better off alone? Or just that no one should settle?"

I take a sip of my beer, feeling the weight of the question. "I think that when people are in relationships, they tend to compromise too much. They lose pieces of themselves. And I think the world convinces women they need love to be fulfilled when really, they just need to trust themselves."

Evie nods, considering. "I get that."

Harper shoots me a look that says, *Do you? Do you get that? Because I don't think you even believe it anymore.* If I believed it so strongly, couldn't I, you know, write about it?!

I shift in my seat, suddenly antsy.

Chase must sense the tension because he claps his hands together and stands. "Alright, enough of the heavy stuff. Who's up for a bonfire?"

I exhale slowly, grateful for the subject change.

Harper grins. "Absolutely."

Evie cheers.

I sigh.

And Chase?

He just smirks.

Because, of course, he knows exactly how to push my buttons.

The bonfire crackles, casting flickering shadows along the beach, and despite every logical bone in my body telling me I *should not be here*, I am, in fact, here.

Sitting cross-legged in a lounge chair, a mostly empty hard seltzer in my hand, I listen to Evie and Harper crack up over some story about a disastrous first date while the warm glow of firelight makes Chase Remington look like something out of a damn summer romance novel.

The worst part?

I keep noticing.

Noticing how his golden skin glows in the fire-light, how his eyes crinkle when he laughs, how his forearms flex as he casually nurses a beer, and how the breeze ruffles his hair just enough to make it look effortlessly perfect.

God, I hate him.

"You're awfully quiet over there, Scottie," Chase drawls, tipping his bottle in my direction, that signature smirk firmly in place.

I roll my eyes. "I just have nothing to contribute to this *riveting* conversation about dates gone wrong."

Harper scoffs. "You have *plenty* of bad date stories."

"I don't *date*," I remind her, taking a sip. "That's the entire foundation of my career, if you recall."

Evie hums, propping her chin on her hand. "That actually leads me to a better idea than first-date horror stories." She grins. "We should play *Never Have I Ever*."

Harper immediately lights up. "*Yes*."

"No," I deadpan.

"Yes," Chase counters, his eyes flashing with amusement. "C'mon, Scarlett. What's the worst that could happen?"

I squint at him. "You want an actual list?"

Evie waves a hand, already too excited about this whole thing. "It's happening. We all know how it works. If you've done it, you drink." She levels a look at me. "No lying."

I sigh dramatically, but everyone else is already on board.

Evie goes first, a classic warm-up. "Never have I ever been arrested."

Harper immediately takes a sip.

We all gape at her.

"What?" she says, laughing. "It was just a *little* trespassing."

Evie grins, and the game continues, bouncing between funny and ridiculous.

Then Chase speaks.

"Never have I ever..." He pauses, his gaze flickering to me. "Fallen for someone I wasn't supposed to."

The air shifts.

I grip my drink a little tighter.

Harper drinks. Evie drinks.

I don't.

And Chase notices.

His smirk turns smug. "No one, huh?"

I arch a brow. "Not all of us make a habit of chasing after bad decisions."

"Shame," he murmurs, tilting his beer to his lips. "Sometimes bad decisions are the most fun."

His voice is *too* smooth, *too* confident, and I hate that my stomach twists in response.

Harper jumps in before I can snap back.

"Never have I ever..." She grins, her eyes flicking to Chase. "Had a *thing* for my neighbor."

Oh, she *would*.

Evie giggles. Chase looks way too pleased with himself.

And me? I keep my drink firmly in my lap.

Chase makes a show of sipping his beer, eyes

locked on mine.

I scowl. "You *don't* have a thing for me."

His smirk deepens. "Never said I did."

I want to throw my drink at him.

I resist, but just barely.

The game goes on, and the more we drink, the more I hate the way my body *reacts* to him.

The way the firelight dances across his face.

The way his voice roughens when he teases me.

The way his eyes flick to my lips when I take a sip of my drink.

I hate him. I *hate* him.

But then—

"Never have I ever been in love," Evie says, her voice softer than before.

A hush falls over the group.

I don't drink.

Chase doesn't drink.

And for the first time all night, we aren't teasing. We aren't bickering.

We're just... looking at each other.

And something shifts.

Something I don't want to name.

I clear my throat, forcing a smirk. "Depressing, Remington. You've never been in love?"

He shrugs, but his expression is unreadable. "I guess I'm just waiting for the right one to change my mind."

The words are light, teasing—just like always.

But his *eyes*?

They're anything but.

I swallow hard, my pulse hammering in my ears.

I need another drink.

I need away from *him*.

But as the fire crackles, and the drinks flow, and Harper and Evie dissolve into laughter beside us, I realize something I really, really don't want to.

For the first time in a long time…

Maybe I'm right where I'm supposed to be.

9

AMBUSHED

Scarlett

I wake up to golden morning light streaming through the bedroom window and the distant sound of waves lapping against the shore. For a few blissful moments, I lie there, warm beneath the covers, stretching lazily and letting my mind drift.

Then the memories hit.

The bonfire. The drinks. Chase.

I groan and drag a pillow over my face. Why did I have to notice him last night? The way his voice roughened when he teased me. The way his smirk made my pulse do stupid things. The way his stupidly golden skin glowed in the firelight.

I blame the alcohol.

Except I'm not hungover. Not even a headache. Meaning I can't even excuse the fluttering feeling in my stomach as the result of one too many hard seltzers. The memory of him drinking me in like I was the most interesting thing at the fire pit settles somewhere deep.

I exhale sharply and shove the covers off. This is fine. I am fine.

Chase is an overconfident hockey player with a face carved by the gods and an ego twice the size of Lake Michigan. I don't even like him. We are not friends. I'm just momentarily experiencing a lapse in judgment due to prolonged exposure. Nothing a little distance can't fix.

I throw on some clothes and shuffle out of my room, desperate for coffee. But the second I step into the kitchen, I hear it.

Click-clack. Click-clack. Click-clack.

Harper's fingers fly across the keyboard at warp speed, her phone wedged between her ear and her shoulder.

"Mmhm… right, but what if we lean into the controversy?" she says, pausing just long enough to grab her coffee mug and take a sip. "Exactly. Make it an event, something people can't resist clicking on."

I pause in the doorway, frowning. "What are you doing?"

Harper jerks upright as if she forgot I existed, spins to face me, and grins. "Oh, you're up! I have the BEST idea."

I narrow my eyes, but she ends her call and launches into a full-on TED Talk.

"Okay, so you know how you've been struggling with your book? And how you may or may not have gone viral for that, uh… super spicy take on romance novels last month?"

I groan. "Harper—"

"No, listen!" She waves me over like an excited toddler who's just built a LEGO masterpiece. "I was talking to a few PR people I know, and we've got a genius plan that will solve all your problems."

"Uh-huh." I grab my coffee, take a long, slow sip, and brace myself. "Do I want to know?"

"Oh, absolutely. You're going to co-host a romance book club."

I nearly spit my coffee. "I'm sorry, WHAT?"

Harper grins, hands in the air like *ta-da!*

I gape at her. "You're joking."

"Nope." She types something into her laptop, then spins it around so I can see an email chain titled Re: The PR Stunt of the Century.

My stomach drops.

"Harper. What the hell is this?"

She plucks the laptop away before I can slam it shut. "It's genius, that's what. Your publisher loves the idea, Stampede PR loves the idea, and—"

I hold up a hand. "Pause. You're telling me the Dallas Stampede—a hockey team—wants me, a woman who has loudly and publicly waged war on romance, to co-host their romance book club?"

Harper beams. "Yep."

Kill me. Just kill me now.

I rub my temples. "For the love of everything holy, why?"

She sighs dramatically. "Because, babe, people eat this stuff up. You and Chase? You're like the human embodiment of enemies to lovers. Your entire brand is 'I don't believe in love,' and his brand is literally 'I will flirt with anything that moves.'"

I shake my head, unable to process this level of insanity. Especially before coffee. "This is the worst idea I've ever heard."

Harper ignores me. "You're trending. People are arguing about whether you're a romance-hating cynic or just haven't met the right guy yet." She wiggles her eyebrows. "And then there's Chase."

I tighten my grip on my coffee mug. "What about him?"

She shrugs, way too casual. "Oh, nothing. Just that he's about to take over as the new face of the book club, and the internet is already shipping you two into oblivion."

I choke. "WHAT?"

Harper grins. "Hashtag #QuinnWilder walked. #ScottieRemington is about to run."

"No." I point an accusing finger at her. "No. Absolutely not."

"Too late," she sings. "The deal's done. It's all

happening."

I slam my coffee down. "And what if I refuse?"

Harper lifts a brow. "Then your publisher will 'strongly suggest' you reconsider your stance on publicity efforts."

I stare at her, speechless.

She grins. "You're in, babe."

I want to scream.

Instead, I close my eyes, inhale deeply, and mentally start drafting my resignation letter from life.

10

THAT'S A TERRIBLE IDEA, WHEN DO WE START?

Chase

I wake up to the sound of a dog snoring directly in my face.

Rip, sprawled across my bed like he owns the place, exhales a long, dramatic sigh, his nose pressed against my shoulder.

I grunt, pushing him away, and scrub a hand over my face. Sunlight filters through the blinds, too bright and too early. I could use another hour of sleep, but the universe has other plans because my phone starts buzzing on my nightstand.

I groan, blindly reaching for it. Drew.

Nope. Not dealing with that yet.

I silence the call and roll onto my back, exhaling slowly as last night flashes through my mind.

The bonfire. The drinks. The way Scarlett sat across from me, firelight dancing in her eyes, her lips curving around a smirk that had my stomach doing some real inconvenient shit.

I shake my head. Nope. Not going there.

Instead, I drag myself out of bed, throw on a T-shirt, and head downstairs, where Evie is already packing her things by the door.

"Hey," she greets, zipping her bag. "Sorry I have to head out early."

I nod, running a hand through my hair. "Did you sleep okay?"

She snorts. "Considering your dog snores? Yeah, not bad."

Rip, now sitting obediently at her feet, wags his tail like the world's most well-behaved pet.

"Yeah, sorry about that," I mutter, grabbing a bottle of water from the fridge.

Evie just grins, then studies me with that way-too-knowing twin gaze that makes me instantly suspicious.

"What?" I ask, twisting the cap off my water.

She shrugs. "Nothing. Just... last night was fun."

I take a sip, nodding. "Yeah."

"You and Scarlett had a *real* interesting dynamic, though."

I nearly choke. "It's too early for this, Evie."

She grins. "I'm just saying. For two people

who claim to hate each other, there was a lot of eye contact."

I scoff, setting my water down. "That's because I was watching her try to control her rage. It was fascinating."

"Uh-huh." She slings her bag over her shoulder. "Whatever you say."

I roll my eyes. "Drive safe, okay?"

She steps forward and squeezes my arm. "I mean it, Chase. She's got walls, sure, but walls don't go up without a reason. Sometimes, the people who push back the hardest are the ones who need someone to stick around."

I stare at her, but she just pats my cheek and winks. "Love you, loser."

"Love you too, nerd."

She laughs, and then she's gone, leaving me standing in my kitchen with way too many thoughts swirling in my head.

I exhale sharply, pick up my phone, and finally call Drew back.

He answers on the first ring. "There he is. Thought you'd died."

I grab my keys and step outside, walking toward the beach. "Nah, just ignoring you."

"Charming as ever. Listen, I won't keep you long, but I've got an interesting proposition for you."

I smirk. "If it's about the book club thing, save

it. Not happening." Bennett already tried to sell me on the same thing…

"Not so fast. We got a call from a publisher today—with an interesting proposal."

I frown. "What kind of proposal?"

A pause. "Bestselling author Scottie Calloway has agreed to co-host this thing with you."

I stop in my tracks.

"I'm sorry, what?"

Rip, completely unaware of my inner turmoil, is taking the world's longest pee in the sand.

"You heard me."

"No, no. I must have misunderstood you. You're telling me that the same Scottie Calloway— the one who's made a career out of telling women they don't need men—is voluntarily signing up for a romance book club?"

"That's the one."

I bark out a laugh. "And this makes sense how?"

"The Stampede's PR team is playing up the 'Enemies to Lovers' angle. Your on-screen bickering will draw an audience. Whether she's right or wrong, whether she's read the right books, whether she's just bitter. It'll create fan engagement, and at the end of the day, that's what this is really about."

I shake my head, pacing along the shoreline. "You really think this is gonna work?"

Drew chuckles. "Oh, it's already working. The

internet is buzzing about you two. The 'romance cynic versus the hockey player who probably writes girls' numbers on napkins' narrative? People love it."

I scowl. "I do not write my number on napkins."

I put them into my phone like a normal guy.

"Not the point."

I scrub a hand over my jaw, my brain still trying to process this. Scarlett. Co-hosting. With me.

I shouldn't be entertained by this. But damn it, I am.

"What do you say, Chase?" Drew asks, amusement clear in his voice. "You in?"

I look out at the lake, the water glinting under the morning sun. I think about Scarlett's smirk last night, the way her pulse kicked up when I got too close, the way her glare burned hot enough to melt steel.

The thought of working with her? Professionally? I'm slightly horrified, slightly turned on.

This can't be happening. Except, apparently, it is.

I grin. "Oh, I'm in."

11

MISSING SOMETHING

Chase

I should be in heaven.

Perfect weather. Miles of open beach. I have nothing but time to work out, sleep, and avoid the firecracker next door.

And yet...

I toss a frisbee down the shoreline for Rip, watching him bolt after it as if his life depends on catching the flimsy piece of plastic. His paws kick up sand, and the late afternoon sun casts everything in a golden glow.

A perfect day. A perfect vacation. So why does it feel like something's missing?

Or, more specifically, someone.

Scarlett.

It's been a full week since I've seen her. A week without any snarky glares over the property line, without her stomping across the sand in another swimsuit or sundress that does insane things to my focus, without her sitting on her deck with a coffee and a scowl.

I should be relieved.

Instead, I'm standing here wondering why the hell I even care.

I roll my shoulders and shake it off. Maybe she left early. Maybe she finally got inspired and is locked away writing. Maybe she found someone else to annoy instead of me.

Whatever the reason, I shouldn't be thinking about it.

And yet—

I toss the frisbee again, watching Rip race off, my mind still circling back to her.

Maybe it's the bonfire night that changed things. I don't know what the hell happened, but for the first time since I met her, Scarlett wasn't just sarcastic and prickly. She was...different. Less armor. More real.

And I liked it.

Which is exactly why I need to get my head on straight.

I head inside, grab a water bottle, and prop my feet on the coffee table. My phone sits face-up next to me, and I thumb through a dozen unread texts from women back home who would happily remind me that Scarlett Calloway is not my problem.

I don't answer a single one.

Instead, I grab the book sitting on my table.

Her book.

I don't even know why I bought it—just to annoy her, probably. But now, I stare at the title—*How to Die Alone (and Love Every Second of It)*—and something about it piques my curiosity. What could it possibly be about?

I flip it open.

I tell myself I'll read one chapter. Just to see what she's peddling. Just so, next time I see her, I can throw one of her own arguments back at her.

But then—

One chapter turns into three.

And by the time I stop, Rip is asleep next to me and my head hurts.

Not because I disagree with her. Because some of what she says makes sense.

And I hate that.

I run a hand down my face.

I need a distraction. A drink. A fight. A game. A woman in my bed. Something.

But instead, I find myself looking out the window at her house—empty porch, untouched deck, no sign of life.

I miss her.

And that frustrates me more than anything.

I rub the back of my neck, then grab my keys. Time to get out of my own head.

Turns out, I don't have to go looking for a distraction.

Because I run straight into one at the coffee shop.

Well, more like she almost runs into me, arms full of two coffees, balancing a bag of something against her ribs.

Scarlett freezes mid-step, barely catching herself before slamming into my chest.

"Oh, for heaven's sake," she mutters under her breath.

Ah. There she is.

The tightness in my chest that I *refuse* to call relief eases slightly.

I lean casually against the counter, smirking. "So, did I scare you off, or did you just need a break from glaring at me every morning?"

Her lips press together. Adorable.

"If only I'd been so lucky," she deadpans. "But no. Just working. Unlike some people, I actually have a job to do."

I arch a brow. "Didn't say you didn't."

Her expression sours.

Here's the thing about Scarlett—poking at her is way too much fun. Because every time I think she's maxed out on irritation, she finds a new level.

"So," I say, "you gonna tell me why you've been avoiding me, or should I just assume it's because you can't stop thinking about me?"

Her death glare is immediate. "I have literally never thought about you once in my life."

I drop my gaze pointedly to the two coffees she's holding. "That for me?"

She exhales sharply and shifts them out of reach.

"You know," I muse, "you're kind of proving my point here."

She scowls. "What point?"

"That you're avoiding me. Like, real effort, full-fledged strategy, radio silence avoidance. I'd almost be impressed if it weren't so obvious."

She huffs. "Don't flatter yourself. I was just busy."

"Oh yeah? Busy with what?"

Her pause is all the answer I need.

I grin. "Yeah. That's what I thought."

Her jaw clenches, but then she forces a fake smile.

"Strange turn of events," I say, meeting her eyes. "Looks like we're stuck hosting a book club together."

"That was all Harper. Just know she's dead to me."

I smirk. "Let's try not to make it awkward."

She scoffs. "You make everything awkward."

"Nah," I say, tilting my head. "You just make everything more fun."

Her eye roll is brutal, but for the first time all

week, I feel like myself again.

I decide to leave her to sulk and head to the counter to order. "See you soon, Calloway."

12

ENEMIES WITH ELECTRICITY

Scarlett

The storm rolls in fast.

One minute, the lake is calm, the sky painted in soft pinks and oranges from the sunset. The next, the temperature drops—that sudden, skin-prickling chill that makes the hair on my arms stand up. The air grows thick and electric, heavy with the metallic scent of approaching rain.

Through the windows, I watch the lake transform from placid blue to angry gray-green, whitecaps forming like bared teeth. A wall of gray clouds barrels in, and the wind starts whipping my patio furniture around the deck. I rush outside, barely managing to drag the chairs closer to the house before the first fat raindrops splatter against my arms—irregular plops that quickly become a deafening drumroll against the roof.

I've just made it back inside when—*boom!*

Thunder doesn't just sound—it vibrates through the floorboards, rattling the dishes in the cupboard. The whole cottage groans against the wind, wood creaking like an old ship at sea.

Then, violent and sudden, another crack of thunder shakes the air, and the power cuts out completely.

I stare into the now pitch-black interior of my house. Are you freaking kidding me?

With a sigh, I grab my phone and turn on the flashlight. I manage to scrounge up a single candle, but no matches.

I grab my laptop, thinking maybe I'll write. The faint glow of the screen is barely enough to see by, but I try to make the best of it.

With the Wi-Fi out, it's actually every writer's dream—the Internet can be a massive distraction.

But my laptop is low on battery, and a warning flashes on the screen. *Great.* I close it. No writing tonight. And no Netflix either. No distractions from my own miserable thoughts.

Maybe it'll come back on soon.

It doesn't.

I give it fifteen minutes, then thirty. Nothing. Just the sound of rain hammering the roof, the wind lashing at the windows. My phone battery is at a tragic 18%, and I left my portable charger in my suitcase. Somewhere in the dark abyss that is my bedroom.

Perfect.

I mutter to myself about how this was supposed to be a peaceful, distraction-free summer. A chance to recharge, to figure out what the hell is wrong with me and why I can't write this damn book. Now, I can't even charge my laptop, let alone my brain.

I grab a blanket, throw myself onto the couch, and try to convince myself that this is fine.

Except it's *not fine.*

Because it's muggy as hell with no AC, my phone is dying, and worst of all… I'm bored.

I pace the small living room, stopping dead in my tracks when I see lights glowing from next door. Chase's house has electricity. I flip the light switch a few times to make sure I'm not losing it.

Nothing. With an irritated groan, I storm over to the door. *Fine.* If the universe wants to screw with me, then I'll screw right back.

I'm going to knock on Chase Remington's door, demand to charge my cell phone, and leave without engaging in a single second of unnecessary conversation.

This is survival. Not some excuse to see him again.

Not at all.

I yank open the front door, immediately regretting everything.

The wind practically body-slams me, sending my hair flying into my face, rain pelting my skin like tiny bullets. I stagger forward, pulling my arms around myself as I stomp across the small stretch of sand and grass to his annoyingly well-lit rental.

I reach the door and hesitate for half a second before knocking.

It swings open almost immediately.

Chase is standing there in sweatpants and a plain T-shirt, looking casual and slightly rumpled. His hair is all messy and tousled, and he looks unfairly good for someone who was probably lounging around doing nothing.

One dark brow lifts. "Lemme guess—you finally missed me too much?"

I cross my arms. "My power's out."

His lips twitch like he's holding back a smile. "And?"

"And do you have a spare room or not?"

He leans against the doorframe, crossing his arms over his broad chest. Smugness practically radiates off of him. He's *thinking*… like I asked him to solve a difficult math equation. *What the actual.*

"Depends. You planning to kill me in my sleep?"

I scowl. "No promises."

He smirks, takes way too long to answer, then finally steps aside. "Come on in. Try not to set anything on fire."

I step past him, muttering, "Like I said, no promises."

The second I step inside, the warmth hits me—a sharp contrast to the cold rain still dripping down my arms. Chase shuts the door behind me, locking out the wind.

I take a deep breath. Wow, it smells good in here. Like fresh laundry and some faint woodsy cologne.

Not that I should care.

Not that I *do* care.

Chase eyes me, his lips twitching like he's barely restraining himself. "So, you just stood in the rain for fun or…?"

I glare. "It's called getting from Point A to Point B, Remington."

He drags his gaze over me, his expression unreadable. "Well, Point B is making a mess of my floor."

I follow his glance and scowl. Damn it. My T-shirt is soaked through, dripping small puddles onto the hardwood. My shorts are damp, and my sneakers squish slightly when I shift my weight.

He sighs and shakes his head. "Hold on."

He disappears down the hallway and returns a few moments later, tossing me a towel and—of all things—a hoodie.

I catch both instinctively, frowning at the fabric

in my hands. It's soft and well-worn, a dark navy with the Stampede logo on the chest.

I lift a brow. "You're really gonna make me wear your team merch?"

Chase smirks, way too pleased with himself. "Think of it as an initiation."

A reminder that I'll be working with him on the team's book club. *Gag.*

I roll my eyes but take the towel and start drying off anyway.

Rip watches us from his spot near the couch.

"Guest room's down the hall if you wanna change."

I debate refusing—on principle—but my soaked clothes are glued to my skin, and I'm not about to sit around in damp discomfort out of sheer spite.

With a dramatic sigh, I grab the hoodie and stomp off to change.

I slip off the wet T-shirt and tug the hoodie on. The damn thing smells like him. Like cedar and soap and something uniquely Chase. Unfair.

I return to the living room with Chase's hoodie drowning me. The sleeves are ridiculously long, the hem falling mid-thigh over my shorts.

Chase takes one look at me and grins.

I thrust the towel at him, and he takes it.

He chuckles but says nothing and hangs the towel over a dining chair. A fire flickers in the fireplace, casting warm light across the space. The storm rumbles outside, but in here, it's almost... cozy.

Chase flops onto the couch, stretching an arm along the back. Like he owns the place. Which, fine. He does.

I hesitate, then lower myself into the chair across from him.

Chase shakes his head, amusement dancing in his eyes. He tips his water bottle to his lips, watching me over the rim.

I ignore the way his stupid forearm flexes.

I definitely ignore the way he's watching me like I'm the most entertaining thing in the room.

This is *not* how I envisioned my night going. Finally, he exhales, setting his water down. "So."

I arch a brow. "So." My gaze drifts to the coffee table.

I freeze.

Blink.

My book.

My book, sitting right there, next to his drink, a worn bookmark peeking out from the middle.

I sit up and reach for it before I even think twice. "Wait. Are you *reading* my book?"

Chase stretches, like this isn't shocking information. "You thought I just bought it to impress you?"

I scowl because *yeah*, that's exactly what I

thought. But I can't say that out loud, so instead, I huff, "I don't know if you've noticed, but I'm *not* that easily impressed."

Chase hums like he's considering that, then shrugs. "Eh. I'll figure out what works eventually."

I flip through the pages, half-expecting them to be crisp and untouched, but no—there are dog-eared corners and subtle creases along the spine. The man has *been reading* this.

"You're *halfway through*." My voice is laced with suspicion. "That's... unexpected."

He shrugs. "It's not bad. A little bleak for my taste, but I'm holding out for the part where you admit love isn't a scam after all."

I snort. "Spoiler alert: that part *doesn't exist.*"

Chase sighs. "Damn. And here I thought it was all just a slow burn to the big romantic realization."

I narrow my eyes at him, gripping the book a little tighter.

His lips twitch.

I close my mouth.

Set the book back down.

Take a deep breath.

I swear he does these things just to mess with me.

"What's the deal with your current book?" he asks.

My stomach tightens. "What do you mean?"

"I mean..." He gestures vaguely. "You've said

you're here to work, and you've been holed up like a gremlin, so how's the book coming along?"

I glare. "I'm not a gremlin."

"You're a little gremlin-y."

I take a breath through my nose. *Do not kill him. This is his house.*

Then I exhale. "Fine. Yes. I'm here to work. And no, I haven't written much."

His eyes narrow slightly, like he's actually thinking this through. "Writer's block?"

I hesitate because it's more than that. But that's the easiest answer, so I nod. "Something like that."

He hums, studying me. It's unnerving.

Then, out of nowhere, he grins. "You know what helps with a creative block?"

I give him a flat look. "If you say 'watching hockey,' I'm leaving."

He snorts. "No. Ice cream."

I blink. "Ice cream?"

He stands, sauntering toward the kitchen like this is just a normal Tuesday.

Maybe it is.

I hesitate for half a second before following.

He pulls a pint of chocolate peanut butter swirl from the freezer and slides it across the counter.

I stare at it.

Then back at him.

I remember fighting over the last pint at the store. "My favorite."

He smirks, grabbing two spoons. "Mine too. And yet, I'm sharing it. Look at me, being the bigger person."

I roll my eyes but grab the pint, popping the lid. "Bare minimum effort, Remington."

He chuckles, pulling himself onto the counter, feet swinging lazily. I try very hard not to look at his thighs.

We eat in silence for a few moments, the storm raging outside while everything inside feels… calm.

Which is weird.

Because Chase is the opposite of calm. He's loud and cocky and the kind of guy who thrives on chaos.

And yet, I feel strangely at ease in his kitchen, stealing bites of his ice cream.

"So." He licks his spoon, and I absolutely don't watch. "You always write books about how love is a scam?"

I bristle. "It's not a scam. It's just a distraction."

Chase raises a brow. "Says who?"

I sigh, setting my spoon down. "Says my entire life experience."

His expression shifts. Just slightly.

Then he exhales, tipping his head against the cabinet. "Yeah. I get that."

I blink, because I didn't expect him to agree. "You do?"

He doesn't answer immediately. Just stares at the ceiling, brows pulled together in thought.

Then—softer than before—he says, "Yeah. I do."

I don't ask what he means.

And for once, he doesn't push me to explain myself either.

For a few minutes, we just exist—eating ice cream, listening to the storm.

We finish the pint of ice cream, and since my house is still completely dark, Chase shows me to the guest room.

I tell myself I'm going to sleep.

I really do.

But sleep doesn't come easy when the wind howls against the windows like a thing possessed, and the rain lashes against the roof in unpredictable bursts.

I shift under the ridiculously nice blankets of his guest room—which is stupidly comfortable—but it doesn't help. My mind is restless, body wired from the night's events, the steady rhythm of the storm, and the sugar I consumed.

Ugh.

I give up, kick off the blankets, and swing my legs over the side of the bed. Maybe if I get some water, it'll help.

But when I step into the hallway, I realize I'm not the only one still awake.

A warm glow spills from the kitchen, and when I turn the corner, there he is.

Chase.

Standing at the window, one hand braced on the counter. He's wearing only a pair of athletic shorts that hang low on his hips. The soft kitchen light makes his shoulders look broader, the muscles in his back impossibly wide as he watches the rain.

Something about it feels... unguarded. Like I'm seeing him in a way I'm not supposed to.

He doesn't turn around, but somehow, he knows I'm there.

"Can't sleep either?" His voice is low, rough from the quiet.

"Not when Mother Nature is out for blood." I move to the counter, grab a glass from his cabinet, and fill it with water.

He huffs a quiet laugh, but he doesn't look away from the window. "Yeah. Storms can be re-lentless out here."

I sip my water, stealing a glance at him over the rim of my glass. His profile is sharp in the dim light—jawline shadowed with scruff, lips slightly parted like he's deep in thought.

"Doesn't bother you?" I ask.

He lifts his own water and takes a slow sip.

"Used to them."

I don't know why I stay. Maybe it's the storm. Maybe it's the fact that I'm already awake. Maybe it's the fact that he's not being *insufferable* for once. Either way, I find myself leaning against the counter beside him, staring out into the rain-soaked night.

We stand in comfortable silence for a while, just listening.

Then, out of nowhere, I hear myself say it.

"I grew up in Chicago. About three hours from here."

He turns slightly, giving me his attention.

I don't know why I keep going. I shouldn't keep going. But the words just… come.

"This place—the rental house—it's the last place I remember my family actually being happy." I exhale slowly. "Before the divorce, before everything fell apart… we had one last summer here."

Chase doesn't interrupt. Doesn't make a joke or some sarcastic remark. He just *listens*.

And somehow, that makes me keep talking.

"I was thirteen. I remember my mom playing music while she cooked breakfast. My dad actually laughing. My brother and I sneaking down to the beach at night, thinking we were getting away with something." I swallow. Exhale. "It was the last time we all felt like a family. The last time I believed in that kind of thing."

Silence stretches between us, thick and charged, but not uncomfortable.

"I'm sorry," he finally says, his voice quiet.

I shrug, stare down at the water glass in my hands. "It was a long time ago."

A beat. Then—

"I was playing in a tournament," Chase says, so suddenly I almost don't register it.

I glance at him, confused. "What?"

He exhales and places his hand on the counter. "When it happened. My brother Owen's accident."

My stomach tightens.

He hasn't talked about his brother much—just the brief mention of him earlier, the fact that he's in a wheelchair. But now, there's something heavy in Chase's voice. Something unspoken pressing at the edges of his words.

"I was sixteen," he continues, eyes fixed on the window. "Off playing in some stupid tournament, doing what I loved, while back home... my little brother's life was changing forever."

I hold my breath.

"When I got back, nothing was the same. The house was different. The way my parents looked at me was different. Not because they blamed me— they never did—but because *I* did." His fingers tighten around the counter. "I wasn't there when he needed me."

"That's not your fault," I say quietly.

He lets out a slow breath. "Yeah. People say that a lot."

My chest aches.

Not because I pity him—Chase Remington would probably slug me if I did—but because I understand.

The weight of something you can't change. The way one moment can fracture everything you thought you knew. The way it lingers, no matter how much time passes.

I don't know what to say. So I just stand there, letting the rain fill the silence between us.

After a moment, he shifts and glances at me. "So, let me get this straight." His lips tilt just slightly. "You hate romance, but your favorite childhood memory is a summer where your parents were blissfully in love?"

I narrow my eyes. "That's not—"

"You hate relationships, but you wrote *four* bestselling books about them?"

"That's different."

"You sure?"

I huff and push off the counter. "You were doing so well at being tolerable. Let's not ruin it now."

Chase grins, watching me go.

But even as I retreat to the guest room and climb back into the annoyingly comfortable bed, I can't shake the feeling that something shifted tonight.

Because for the first time since meeting him…
I don't *totally* hate Chase Remington.

13

PANCAKES & SELF-CARE

Chase

It's late—almost midnight—and Rip is taking his sweet time sniffing around the bushes, deciding where to relieve himself before we call it a night. The air is cool, and the lake is still.

I glance to my left and see the lights are still on at Scarlett's house.

Through her window, I see her sitting at the dining table, her laptop open in front of her.

I lean against the porch railing, arms crossed as Rip does his thing. She's completely still, staring at the screen, and for a moment, I think—oh, she's up late writing. But then I look closer.

She's not writing.

She's *crying*.

A deep, aching kind of crying—the kind that happens when you're alone and don't think anyone's watching.

Shit.

I shift my weight and glance away. This isn't my business. I should turn around, walk inside, and pretend I didn't see anything.

I *should*.

But I don't.

Instead, I find myself moving toward her house, my feet carrying me across the sand-dusted wooden deck as if it's out of my control. I don't even know what I'm going to say—I just knock.

Soft, but firm.

A few seconds later, the door swings open, and Scarlett blinks up at me, her eyes red-rimmed and her lips parted in surprise.

"You okay?" I ask.

She exhales, her walls snapping into place so fast I almost believe I imagined the tears. "Just great."

Lie.

"Anything I can do?"

She hesitates, fingers tightening around the doorframe, and for a moment, I think she might actually let me in. Let me help. But then she shakes her head. "Sorry, no. I'm just…frustrated."

I lift a brow. "With?"

She sighs and rubs a hand over her forehead. "There's this book critic who posted a scathing review."

I frown. "Like, online?"

"Yeah." She lets out a humorless laugh. "Called me bitter, unoriginal, and exhausting. Suggested maybe I should stop writing about relationships altogether since I clearly hate them so much."

My jaw tightens. "Tell me who it is. I'll find him and kick his ass."

That gets a real laugh out of her—a small, tired one, but a *real* laugh.

"You're gonna fight a literary critic, Remington?" she teases, swiping at the corner of her eye.

"Damn right I am. All I need is a name."

She shakes her head, but there's a tiny ghost of a smile there now. The tension in her shoulders eases just the slightest bit, and for some reason, that makes my chest feel lighter.

Things have shifted between us the tiniest amount since the night of the power outage—since the night I shared about Owen and she told me about her parents' divorce.

There's a pause, then—before I can overthink it—I say, "Come on."

She frowns. "Come on where?"

"Let's go get something to eat." Food always makes me feel better, and I'm out of other ideas.

Scarlett stares at me like I've lost my mind.

"It's midnight."

"There's a twenty-four-hour diner like ten minutes from here." I shrug. "Are you really going to go back inside and stare at that stupid review all night?"

She chews on her bottom lip. I can *see* her hesitating, debating whether or not to let herself say yes.

And then, to my surprise, she does.

"Fine," she mutters, stepping back inside to grab her shoes.

We take my rental Jeep; Scarlett fiddles with the radio while I drive. She finds a classic rock station and leaves it. It's from Pink Floyd's Dark Side of the Moon. She has good taste.

"Serious question," I say. "Would you ever want to go to space?"

"Not my vibe. I like the earth and think I'm good here."

I nod. "That's fair."

"Plus I would probably barf," she announces.

I chuckle.

The roads are quiet, and we reach the diner in minutes. It's the only place still open in town, a neon *OPEN* sign flickering in the window as I pull into the lot.

Inside, it's all checkered floors and vinyl booths, the faint hum of a jukebox playing an old country song in the corner. The scent of coffee and grease fills the air, and Scarlett slides into a booth across from me, eyeing the laminated menu.

A waitress with a nametag that says *Doris*

strolls over, not even bothering to ask for our order.

"Two stacks of pancakes, side of bacon," she says, jotting it all down. "And an order of fries—extra crispy—with a side of ranch."

Scarlett and I blink at her.

"How'd you do that?" Scarlett asks.

"I have a knack for guessing people's orders," Doris says with a shrug.

"Works for me," I say.

"Me too," Scarlett adds.

"You want coffee?"

Scarlett nods.

"Black," I say. "Decaf."

Doris smirks. "Figures."

Scarlett watches her walk away, both of us still a bit stunned.

"So," I say, leaning back in the booth. "Do you usually read your book reviews, or do you tend to ignore them?"

She exhales through her nose, eyes narrowing slightly. "A mix of both, I guess. When a book first releases, I like to hear how people perceive it. What they think of the thing I spent months of my life working on. Then I tend to let it go. It's not like I can change anything after the fact if everyone hates it."

I lift a brow. "Then why let this guy get under your skin?"

Her lips press together, but I don't miss the

slight flicker of amusement in her eyes. "Valid. It's just that he has a huge following, so it feels extra tragic. Like I was publicly roasted or something."

"Yeah, well, people love running their mouths about things they don't understand," I say, lifting my coffee. "Happens in hockey all the time. Some dude with an X account and a Cheeto-dusted keyboard thinks he knows the game better than the guys who've spent their whole lives playing it."

Scarlett hums, tracing the rim of her water glass. "And what do you do when that happens?"

"Easy." I smirk. "I score goals and prove them wrong."

She snorts, shaking her head. "Well, unfortunately, I can't just body-check my critics into the boards."

"Could be entertaining."

"Pretty sure my publisher would frown upon it."

I tilt my head, studying her. "You really care what they think, huh?"

Scarlett shifts in her seat, reaching for her coffee. "I care when they get it *wrong.*"

Before I can respond, Doris returns with our food, setting down two massive plates of pancakes, crispy bacon, and an order of fries. It's weird, but it works.

She lifts a brow at the portion size. "You trying to bribe me with food, Remington?"

"Depends. Is it working?" I grin, picking up the can of whipped cream and the syrup and adding both to my pancakes.

She stares in horror. "Remington."

"What?" I say innocently, adding just a little more for good measure. "Try it."

We're somewhere between breakfast and dessert.

"This is a calorie bomb." She scoffs, giving her pancakes the same treatment when I pass her the whipped cream and syrup.

I shrug. "No, it's self-care."

Scarlett smiles, like she *wants* to be mad, like she *wants* to push me away, but she can't quite fight it.

Because she's tired. Because she's frustrated. Because, whether she likes it or not, she *needed* this—needed to get out of her own head for a few hours.

I watch as she picks up her fork, scoops up an obnoxious amount of whipped cream, and takes a bite.

Her eyelids flutter slightly, a small sound of reluctant approval slipping from her lips.

I grin.

14

STAY IN YOUR LANE

Scarlett

I agree to go to the dog park for one reason and one reason only—Rip.

It has nothing to do with Chase. Nothing to do with the way my stomach twisted when he texted me, "Rip wants to go run. You coming?" Definitely nothing to do with the way my fingers hesitated over my phone before I typed back a reluctant, "Fine."

It's because I love Rip. That's all.

The park itself is more of a winding trail than a fenced-in enclosure. It stretches along the dunes, weaving through shaded pockets of oak trees where the air is cool and damp, smelling of moss and old leaves. The trail is a mixture of packed sand and pine needles that muffle our footsteps, while wild blackberry bushes crowd the path in places, their thorns catching at our clothes.

When the trees finally part to reveal the lake, the temperature drops by five degrees instantly. The breeze carries the sound of waves and the faint diesel smell of a distant freighter, mixing with the fresh water scent. It's beautiful and peaceful—the perfect place for a person to clear their head. Or, in Rip's case, to sprint at full speed like he's being chased by demons.

He takes off the second Chase unclips his leash, a blur of golden fur and uncontainable energy.

"Wow, does he have an off switch?" I ask.

Chase smirks, watching his dog bolt down the trail. "Only after he's burned through an entire tank of gas. Then he naps like the dead."

I hum, adjusting my sunglasses as we start walking. The sun is out in full force today, the air warm but not too humid, the scent of fresh pine and lake breeze filling the air. It should be relaxing. It should be exactly what I need to clear my head.

But my brain won't shut up.

I keep thinking about the past few nights, sharing ice cream and pancakes and late-night conversations.

I hadn't planned to let my guard down. Hadn't meant to tell him about my family or how this beach town is the last place I remember my parents being truly happy. But Chase had just… listened. No teasing, no witty comebacks—just quiet, genuine understanding. And then, before I could process that, he told me about Owen.

The way his voice had gone rough when he admitted he wasn't there when his little brother's life changed forever. The guilt he carried. The way he tried to play it off, but I could still hear it in his voice.

We're the same, I'd thought. Both of us running from things, both pretending we don't need anyone.

And that realization had scared the absolute hell out of me.

Because if Chase and I are alike, then maybe—just maybe—I could be wrong.

Wrong about love. Wrong about connection. Wrong about everything I've built my career preaching.

No. I shake the thought off before it can take root.

"Earth to Calloway," Chase says, nudging my elbow. "You good?"

I blink, jolting back to the present. "Yeah, fine."

His eyes flick to mine, assessing. "That was the least convincing answer I've ever heard."

"Congrats," I deadpan. "You've cracked the case."

He huffs a laugh, then gestures ahead. "C'mon. Rip's waiting."

Sure enough, Rip has paused up ahead on the

trail, sitting in the shade of a tree with his tail wagging while he waits patiently for us.

"Who's the best boy?" I coo, rubbing his head while his tongue flops out.

Rip sprints off again, and we dutifully follow.

It's… nice. Surprisingly easy.

Then, just as I start to think we might actually make it through this entire outing without Chase annoying the hell out of me, he asks, "So, how's the writing coming?"

I stiffen.

Damn it.

And just like that, the easy mood evaporates.

Between Harper's constant texts and Chase checking in… I'm ready to snap.

Chase notices immediately. Of course he does.

He arches a brow, oblivious—or maybe not—to the sudden tension in my shoulders. "That bad, huh?"

I exhale slowly, keeping my voice even. "It's fine."

"You hesitated."

"No, I didn't."

He gives me a look. "Scottie…"

I clench my jaw. Why did he have to say my name like that? Like he actually cares?

I force a shrug, adjusting my sunglasses. "It's just… slow-going."

He hums, unconvinced. "Writer's block?"

"No."

"Uh-huh."

I glance at him, scowling. "Do you always have to push?"

His mouth tips into an infuriating smirk. "Yes."

I huff, kicking a loose rock with the toe of my sneaker. "It's not writer's block. It's just… my process."

"Your process," he echoes, sounding uncertain.

I glare at him. "I guess so."

It didn't used to be this way. The old me could whip a book out in six months, *four* if I was really in the zone. I've been struggling for ten now and don't even have a thousand words.

Chase grins, like he enjoys pissing me off. (Spoiler: He does.) Then, in an easy, nonchalant voice, he asks, "So what's the big deal?"

I blink. "What?"

"The writing," he says. "Why do you think you're stuck?"

I scoff. "If I knew that, I wouldn't be stuck."

"Maybe you're overthinking it."

I roll my eyes. "Wow. Thank you, Dr. Remington. Clearly, I just needed a hockey player to mansplain writing to me."

He chuckles, unbothered. "I'm just saying—if you're struggling, maybe don't make it so hard on yourself. Just sit down and write."

I stop walking.

He takes another step before realizing I'm no longer beside him. When he turns back, I cross my arms over my chest. "Oh. Oh, just sit down and write? That's your advice?"

Chase shrugs. "Yeah?"

I stare at him for a long beat. "That is possibly the dumbest thing I've ever heard."

His smirk grows. "You sure? 'Cause I've said a lot of dumb things."

I scowl, planting a hand on my hip. "You think writing is easy, don't you?"

"I didn't say that."

"But you do."

He tilts his head, weighing my words. "I just think if something's important to you, you do the damn thing. Whether it's easy or not."

Something in my chest twists. Annoyance. Frustration. The tiniest shred of self-doubt.

I shake it off.

"You don't get it," I say flatly.

Chase watches me, too perceptive for his own good. "Is it something more? Like you've lost your love for writing?" I open my mouth. Shut it. My pulse kicks up. "You have, haven't you?"

I don't respond.

Because I don't want to say the words out loud.

Because if I do, that means they're real.

The book. My career. Everything I've built.

What if I don't believe in it anymore?

The thought makes my stomach churn.

He studies me for a long beat, then shakes his head. "I think that's your problem, Calloway."

My spine stiffens. "What?"

"You're scared."

I scoff. "Of what?"

He takes a slow step toward me, eyes never leaving mine. "That you don't believe in what you're writing anymore."

"Where are you getting this stuff?" I force out a laugh, but it comes out flat, off-sounding.

"I don't know. I just think maybe it's not your fault; maybe there's a reason why you're struggling."

"Oh, please… enlighten me then."

He turns to meet my eyes. "Maybe your problem is that you don't actually believe the stuff you preach."

I go still.

A cold breeze rolls in from the lake, but it's nothing compared to the way my blood runs hot.

How dare he?

What the hell does he know about any of this?

I don't think. I don't hesitate. I just snap.

"Why don't you stay in your lane, and I'll stay in mine? I know nothing about hockey, and you know nothing about writing."

He nods. "I don't know anything about writing, you're right. But I do know that you're struggling.

And at some point, you have to stop blaming other people for why you're so freaking miserable."

The words hang between us like a loaded gun.

Chase's jaw tightens. A muscle in his cheek twitches.

I see red. How dare he pretend to know what I'm thinking, what I feel?

We met two weeks ago.

"Have fun with Rip," I say. "I'm going to walk back."

And without waiting for his response, I turn and head for the water. It's probably a mile back to my house.

15

CLASSIC REMINGTON

Chase

So… I messed up. Pretty badly.

I stare out at the waves crashing against the shore. Rip lies at my feet, snoring softly, blissfully unaware of the absolute wreck I've made of things.

"I put my nose where it didn't belong and said some things that angered Scarlett," I continue, phone pressed to my ear. "If I could take it back, I would. She's not speaking to me, and I haven't seen her in a week."

There's a beat of silence before Evie sighs dramatically. "Chase."

"I know."

"No, you don't know. Because if you did, you wouldn't have done whatever stupid thing you did to make her mad."

I groan and let my head fall back against the deck railing. "It wasn't even that bad."

"Uh-huh. And yet, you haven't seen her in a week?"

I scowl. "It's not my fault she's actively avoiding me."

Evie hums, and I can practically hear her amused little smirk through the phone. "Are you sure? Maybe she just realized she needs a break from your relentless charm."

I grunt. "If that were the case, she wouldn't have lasted more than two days."

She snorts. "You sound like you miss her."

I kick at a loose plank on the deck, watching as Rip twitches in his sleep. "I don't *miss* her."

Evie lets out a sharp laugh. "That was the least convincing thing you've ever said."

I glare at the water like it personally offends me. "It's just… weird. After the power outage, the storm, the ice cream, I thought…"

I trail off because I don't really know what I was thinking.

That we were friends? That we'd actually started to enjoy each other's company? That maybe— just maybe—I was finally getting under her skin in a way that wasn't just pure irritation?

I shake my head, frustrated.

"Forget it," I mutter. "Doesn't matter. Michigan's almost over. We've got one book club thing in Dallas, and then we'll go our separate ways."

Evie scoffs. "Yeah, sure. Because working together in front of a million eyes is gonna be *so* easy when she's still pissed at you."

I rub my temple. "I never said it was gonna be easy."

"She's still pissed?"

"I'm assuming so. Did you miss the part where I said I haven't seen her in seven days?"

Evie clicks her tongue. "And you haven't tried to fix it?"

"I can't exactly *force* her to talk to me. She's stubborn as hell."

"Well, duh. That's why you like her."

I still.

My heart kicks up.

Evie doesn't say anything for a beat, letting the words settle.

I scowl. "I don't *like* her."

She hums. "Mmm. Okay."

"Evie."

"Chase."

I groan, scrubbing a hand over my jaw. "I *don't.*"

"Right. And I'm sure you're totally fine never seeing her again after this whole book club thing wraps up."

I grind my teeth.

Evie *definitely* hears my silence because she

laughs.

"Oh my gosh," she says. "You *do* like her."

I pinch the bridge of my nose. "I'm hanging up now."

"Fine, fine. Just do me a favor?"

I sigh. "What?"

"Fix it."

I let my head fall back against the railing again and stare up at the sky.

Yeah.

Easier said than done.

Bennett Wilder lives in a house that looks like it belongs on one of those fancy home renovation shows—big windows, sprawling backyard, the kind of kitchen that probably cost more than my entire rookie contract. It's a step up from the downtown condo he used to own when we were roommates, but I guess that's what happens when you settle down, get married, and start popping out kids.

"Come on in, Uncle Chase!" Lucy says, pulling the door open with a grin.

I step inside and am immediately met with the sound of toddler squeals. Their son Theo—two years old and full of chaos—comes barreling toward me with all the force of a charging bull. I crouch just in time to catch him, scooping him up before he can crash into my nuts.

"Buddy, you gotta work on that stopping thing," I say, ruffling his mop of curls.

He grins up at me, all dimples and trouble. "Chase go fast!"

Bennett strolls in from the kitchen, wiping his hands on a dish towel, shaking his head. "Great. He's already associating you with speed and recklessness. Just what I need."

I smirk, setting Theo back on his feet. "Can't fight genetics, Wilder."

Lucy, who has been standing nearby with a hand on her belly, snorts. "This baby is going to inherit my coordination."

Bennett slings an arm around her waist and kisses her cheek. "Baby, you once tripped over *air* in our kitchen."

Lucy shoves him away with an affectionate glare. "I was distracted."

He smirks. "By me?"

She rolls her eyes. "By *hunger*."

They're disgusting. I hate them.

Lucy waddles back to the kitchen, rubbing her belly. "Make yourself at home, Chase. Dinner's almost ready."

"You mean *I* made dinner," Bennett corrects, grabbing a beer from the fridge.

Lucy waves a hand. "You're good at it. I'm

growing a *human*."

I shake my head, watching them bicker like this is the best part of their day.

Lucy Quinn, formerly known as the Queen of Hockey Social Media, somehow went from being the bane of Bennett's existence to the love of his life.

It's weird seeing one of your best friends *happy*. Like, *domestic* happy. It used to freak me out. But now?

I dunno.

It doesn't freak me out as much as it used to.

Dinner is full of the usual—Bennett trying to get Theo to eat his veggies, Lucy failing miserably at pretending to help, and the two of them tag-teaming me about my off-season.

It's to be expected.

"So," Lucy starts, pouring herself a ginger ale. "You went off the grid for a while there. No wild parties? No random hookups making headlines? No Chase Remington 'Bad Boy' antics?"

I sigh. "Nice to see you, Luce. Always a pleasure."

Bennett snickers. "She's not wrong, man. Usually, we have at least one *What Did Chase Do Now* moment before training camp."

"I went home for the summer," I say, shrugging. "Got a beach rental in Michigan. Worked out, relaxed, spent time with my family."

Lucy raises a brow. "Relaxed? You?"

Bennett smirks. "Let me guess. Lasted two weeks before you got bored out of your damn mind?"

I stab a piece of steak. "More like three."

Lucy grins. "Impressive."

I take a sip of beer. "Not much else to report. Now I'm back, getting ready for the season."

"*And* co-hosting a book club with a famous author," Bennett points out, leaning back in his chair.

Lucy perks up. "Oh my gosh, *that's* right. You're working with Scottie Calloway."

"Your guess is as good as mine for how it's gonna go," I say, shaking my head. "Should be interesting, to say the least."

Bennett eyes me, suspicious. "Interesting?"

Lucy narrows her gaze. "That's an *understatement* if I've ever heard one. Her whole thing is anti-romance, right? 'Women don't need men' and all that?"

"Yep."

"And *you* are literally hockey's biggest flirt."

"Also correct."

Lucy leans forward, eyes twinkling. "Chase. Please tell me you're going to take this seriously."

"I intend to, but here's the thing…she kind of hates me."

Lucy exchanges a look with Bennett, then tilts her head. "What'd you do?"

Does it annoy me that they assume I did something wrong? *Greatly.* Am I surprised? *Not a bit.*

I take another sip of my beer.

"She probably hates all men," Lucy waves me off.

Bennett snickers. "Oh yeah. This is gonna be *fun* to watch."

16

NOT BUYING WHAT YOU'RE SELLING

Scarlett

After spending a month in Michigan, coming back to my condo feels... off.

Too quiet.

Too empty.

Too much space for my own thoughts.

It barely feels like home anymore. It should. It's where my career exploded, where I built a life exactly how I wanted it—on my terms, with no distractions, no messy emotions, no heartbreak.

I used to love this. The solitude. The freedom of it. My walls are lined with books, my pantry is stocked with my favorite overpriced organic snacks, and my espresso machine is the closest thing I have to a committed relationship. It's perfect.

Except it's not.

My deadline is creeping closer, but I can't seem to force the words out. Every sentence I type feels hollow.

Because if I put pen to paper—if I actually push ahead on this book—I have to answer a question I don't want to touch with a ten-foot pole.

Do I even believe in what I'm writing anymore?

A sharp knock on my door makes me jolt, but when I check, it's just a package. Something I ordered from Amazon. A pair of Spanx for tonight.

I grab the package, toss it onto my coffee table, and check the time.

5:16 p.m.

The book club event is at seven.

Which means I have less than two hours before I have to sit next to Chase and pretend I don't want to strangle him with his own mic cord.

The thought alone sends a ripple of something through me—annoyance, frustration... something else I refuse to name.

Because the truth is?

I wish he wasn't such a *complete* jerk.

Because if he weren't, I might have to admit he's...

Ugh. No. Not going there.

I shove the thought away and head to my bathroom. My reflection stares back at me, hair knotted in a messy bun, dark circles under my eyes.

I sigh and turn on the shower.

If I'm going to walk into battle tonight, I might as well look the part.

An hour and a half later, I step out of my car, heels clicking against the pavement as I stride toward the event venue. The second I walk through the doors, I catch my reflection in the floor-to-ceiling windows. The navy wrap dress is a good choice—sharp, sophisticated, shows just enough leg to be *dangerous*. My glossy hair frames my face in soft waves, and the lipstick I picked? A bold merlot color.

I *do* look like a woman ready for battle.

I roll my shoulders back and take a breath.

I can do this.

I can sit next to Chase Remington, debate romance novels, and not let him get under my skin.

I can ignore the way my stomach tightens when I think about seeing him again, how even now, my pulse kicks up a little in anticipation.

I *can*.

And I *will*.

Because at the end of the day, this is just another PR stunt.

And Chase Remington?

He's just another opponent.

I expected a small crowd—a handful of die-hard book club members, maybe some Stampede fans who just wanted to see a hockey player fumble his way through a discussion about romance.

What I did *not* expect was a packed house.

The venue is *buzzing*—women of all ages chatting excitedly, clutching copies of books to their chests, sipping on themed cocktails from the cash bar.

I scan the crowd, mildly horrified.

It's not just *big*. It's *huge*.

Do these people *know* I don't actually *like* romance novels? That I, in fact, built my entire career writing about why women don't need men?

And yet, they're *here*.

For this.

For *us*.

God help me.

Before I can turn around and fake an emergency, a woman with sleek dark hair and a professional no-nonsense energy approaches me, clipboard in hand.

"Scarlett Calloway," she says smoothly. "I'm Vivian Carter. Stampede PR."

Oh. *Right*.

I shake her hand, trying not to let my nerves show. "Nice to meet you."

Vivian's gaze sweeps over me, sharp and assessing. "Glad to have you on board for this. I have to say, the online buzz has been fantastic. The whole *'enemies to lovers'* angle? The fans *love* it."

I blink. "I—wait. What angle?"

Vivian just smiles. "Don't worry, you'll catch

on. Chase is already here, by the way. I'll take you to him."

Chase is already here.

I swallow, ignoring the way my stomach twists.

I haven't seen him in weeks. Since *the fight* we had at the dog park.

I've spent the last week telling myself that our time together was just a blip, a brief lapse in judgment on my part. That whatever... *thing* had been happening between us was just proximity, a result of being neighbors in a small town for too long.

But now, standing here, surrounded by hundreds of people waiting for us to take the stage, I know the truth.

I'm *not* over it.

And the second I see him—I *know* I was lying to myself.

Because *wham!*

The air is sucked straight from my lungs.

Gone are the board shorts and flip-flops.

Gone is the too-casual, beach-bum Chase.

The man standing across the room is all sharp edges and tailored lines.

The charcoal-gray suit fits his frame unfairly well, emphasizing every broad, muscular inch of him. He looks even broader and taller than I remember, with his shoulders stretching against the suit jacket. His hair is freshly cut, styled just enough to be polished but still just a *little* messy in the front, like he ran his hand through it before walking in.

And the scruff?

Gone.

Completely clean-shaven, revealing a strong, chiseled jaw that makes my brain short-circuit for a second.

Not fair. Not fair. Not fair.

He turns just as Vivian and I approach, his sharp blue eyes locking onto mine. And damn him—his whole face lights up like we're old friends, like I *didn't* storm off and avoid him for an entire week.

"Scarlett," he says, his voice warm and familiar.

I freeze.

Vivian is still talking, but I don't hear a word she says.

Because Chase Remington—*annoying, cocky, insufferable* Chase—is looking at me like he *enjoys* the fact that I'm flustered.

And worse?

He's right.

I *am* flustered.

I clear my throat, struggling to pull myself together. "You clean up well, Remington."

His lips twitch, and he steps closer, his voice low. "You look… incredible."

Oh.

Okay.

A *real* compliment.

Not teasing. Not sarcasm.

Just—*real*.

I blink up at him, caught off guard by the shift in tone, the sincerity in his eyes. Before I can come up with a snarky comeback to the weird little flutter in my chest, a woman in a glittery blue dress cuts between us.

"Oh my *gosh*—you're Chase Remington, right?" She beams up at him, already pulling out her phone. "Do you mind if I get a picture? My sister and I are huge fans. She's gonna freak."

Chase blinks, then gives her the megawatt smile I've come to associate with his media face. "Of course. I'm happy to."

He shifts easily into charm mode—arm slung casually around her shoulders, dimples flashing, head tilted just right for the selfie. He even laughs when she playfully pokes his chest and says, "You really *are* built like a tank."

And it's stupid.

It's *so* stupid.

But something tightens in my chest.

I glance away, folding my arms across my body like that might help shield me from the weird jolt of… whatever this is.

Jealousy?

God. No.

I don't get jealous. That's not who I am. I'm the

poster girl for independence. The queen of emotional detachment. I literally built a career on the idea that needing a man is a social construct and feelings are, at best, wildly overrated.

But now?

Now, I can't stop watching the way Chase's eyes crinkle when he smiles. The way he's so easy with strangers. The way he slips effortlessly into people's hearts like it's nothing.

I hate it.

I hate that he's good at this.

I hate that I'm suddenly wondering how many other women he's smiled at like that. How many others he's made feel special.

And I *really* hate that I care.

The woman thanks him and floats off with her selfie like she's won the damn lottery. Chase turns back to me, that same grin still hovering on his face—until he sees mine.

"You okay?" he asks, brow furrowing slightly.

"Fine," I say too fast. "Just ready to get this over with."

He studies me for a second like he can see straight through the lie. Then, thankfully, the stage manager calls out that it's time to mic up.

A tech assistant begins clipping mics to us—his on his collar and mine on my dress near my collarbone.

I keep my eyes forward.

Breathe.

I don't have time to analyze it. Because Vivian is leading us toward the stage, and suddenly, it's happening.

The book club event is *starting*.

And I have *absolutely* no idea how I'm going to survive it.

I smooth my hands over my dress for the eighth time and remind myself that I've been on a stage before. I've spoken at events, led panels, and signed books for hours. This is nothing new.

Except it is. Because tonight I'm *not* in a room full of Scottie Calloway superfans. I'm in enemy territory—empowered book club devotees. Like they have dreams of falling in love with their own cinnamon roll hockey player.

Gross.

And unfortunately, I'm the cynic sent here to talk to them about love.

Fantastic.

"I think I might puke," I mutter, mostly to myself.

"Please don't," a voice says, warm and low right by my ear. "It would really ruin the mood."

I flinch, glancing over my shoulder.

Chase.

His voice is filled with both warmth and humor.

The beach bro energy is gone, and somehow that sets me on edge. His tie is slightly loosened, like he's already conquered the day.

He looks... unfairly good.

"I hope you're up for a challenge," he says, eyes gleaming.

I arch a brow. "I can't wait to prove you wrong."

He just grins, like we're about to compete in a game neither of us knows the rules to, but he's convinced he'll win.

I turn away and try not to let his aftershave fry my last functioning brain cell. I adjust the mic clipped to my collar, still in awe of the sheer volume of hopeless romantics on the other side of the curtain.

I exhale and plant a hand on my hip. "Romance novels have never enhanced one person's life. Not one. I can guarantee it. Reading about some bull-riding Fabio or a single dad Navy SEAL and then coming home to your real-life chonky, farting husband who's asking, 'What's for dinner?' Ludicrous. *Nope*. Not here for it. Not buying what you're selling."

"*Scarlett!*" Vivian skids around the corner, her eyes wide with horror. "Your mic is on!"

Oh. No. *No, no, no, no, no.*

I freeze, my blood going ice cold.

"Stage in thirty seconds!" someone yells.

My stomach drops to the floor.

Chase chokes on a laugh beside me. "You really know how to make an entrance, Calloway."

I am going to kill him.

We walk out onto the stage to thunderous applause, and I'm fifty shades of mortified. The lights are blinding, the crowd massive, and the only thing keeping me upright is sheer adrenaline and Chase's annoyingly steady presence beside me.

He steps up to the mic first, flashing his trademark smile. "Hey, everyone. I'm Chase Remington, right wing for the Dallas Stampede and apparently a newfound lover of books."

Low laughter ripples through the audience.

"And I'm Scottie Calloway," I say, trying not to wince. "Thanks for having us."

Someone in the back yells, "We heard you backstage!"

The entire room erupts.

Chase leans toward me and murmurs, "Smile, Calloway. You're charming as hell when you're on the defensive."

I send him a death glare, but somehow, he keeps things moving. He's good at this. Damn him. He tosses out jokes, mentions his favorite book from the club so far, and even manages to redirect the crowd's attention away from me and my mic mishap.

The moderator asks us both, "What's your favorite romance trope?"

"None of them," I grumble.

Chase flashes his signature smile at the crowd,

like they're in on some secret with him. "Enemies to lovers, obviously." Then he smirks directly at me.

Do not commit murder. Do not commit murder.

We settle into a rhythm, him bantering, me offering sarcastic counterpoints, and for a while, it almost feels like fun. Or at the very least, like I might survive this encounter.

Then the Q&A starts.

A woman stands, maybe mid-thirties, holding the mic with both hands. She's got a sweet face and a pink Stampede hoodie on.

"Hi," she says, smiling nervously. "This is for Scottie Calloway. First of all, I love your work— I really do. But... I just wanted to say, I've been married six years. My husband and I? We're both a little chonky. And yeah, sometimes he farts during movies. But there's something kinda nice about being comfortable enough to let one rip here and there. He also holds my hand when I'm anxious and warms up my car on cold mornings. And romance novels? They remind me why I fell in love with him in the first place."

The room goes quiet.

She swallows, steeling herself to continue. "I know they're fiction. I know they're not real life. But they make me happy. They give me hope. And... I don't know. That's not so bad, right?"

She sits.

And the room explodes in applause.

I just… sit there.

Stone-faced and quietly reeling.

All my carefully constructed arguments, all my witty retorts, every armor-plated piece of logic I've used to defend my worldview—it all wobbles.

Like a game of Jenga about to go sideways.

I try to say something. Anything. But the only thing I can manage is a tight-lipped nod.

Chase leans toward his mic. "I think what Scarlett meant earlier—when she was mocking farting husbands—is that she just hasn't met the right one yet."

Laughter again. More applause. Of course, Chase knew exactly what to say to diffuse the situation.

And now, of course, everyone is looking at us like we're one of those *will they or won't they* couples from a slow-burn rom-com.

I want to slide off this stage and never be seen again.

As we wrap things up, Chase turns toward me one last time.

"Well," he says, his voice pitched just loud enough to carry. "You didn't set the place on fire. I call that a win."

I shoot him a look. "Don't tempt me, Remington."

But my voice comes out shaky. Because I'm

off my game. Way off.

And he knows it.

His smirk softens. Just slightly.

And somehow, that's even worse.

Because for the first time in a very long time…
I don't know if I'm the one in control.

17

SHIP HAPPENS

Chase

Scarlett's still red in the face as we step off stage, her jaw tight, arms crossed like she's physically holding herself together.

I've seen people rattled before—hell, I've been rattled plenty of times—but this? This is a woman trying really hard to pretend she's fine when she's absolutely not.

It does something inside me. Some weird nagging feeling that I can't place, but don't like.

She doesn't say anything, just beelines toward the backstage hallway like she's trying to outrun her own embarrassment.

I follow her. Not because I'm an idiot, though the jury's still out. But because I don't like the way her shoulders are pulled tight, like she's bracing for another punch. She's been dodging me all night—

hell, all summer. But tonight? She let a crack show.

And maybe I'm not supposed to care. But I do.

When I catch up to her by the green room door, she stops but doesn't turn around. "Don't say it."

"Say what?" I ask, holding back a smile.

"I don't want to talk about the hot take from hell. I just want to forget this entire night."

"That's fair," I say gently. "But can we talk about tacos?"

That gets her. She glances over her shoulder, narrowing her eyes. "Tacos?"

I shrug. "I know a spot. It's divey. Greasy. Has margaritas the size of your head. It's impossible to feel bad about yourself when you're elbows-deep in barbacoa and tequila."

She blinks at me, like she can't quite compute this version of me. The one offering comfort instead of banter.

"You're inviting me to eat tacos?"

"I'm inviting you to not go home and replay tonight in your head until you hate yourself."

She hesitates. "Do they have chips?"

"Endless," I say solemnly.

A beat of silence.

"Fine. But only because I'm starving."

Twenty minutes later, we're tucked into a booth at

my favorite taqueria just outside downtown. The kind of place where the furniture doesn't match, the salsa is molten lava, and the margaritas taste like they've been spiked with pure happiness.

In a word, it's heaven.

Scarlett's curled into the booth across from me, hair falling over her shoulder, salt glistening on the rim of her glass as she takes a sip and lets out a soft, "Oh, damn. That's good."

I grin. "Told you. Tacos fix everything."

"I didn't say they fixed everything," she says, eyeing me over the glass. "I said the margarita was good."

She's relaxing. Not by a lot. But her shoulders are a little looser. Her voice isn't quite so sharp. She hasn't once looked at her phone.

I reach for a chip. "You know, I expected you to bail after tonight."

She snorts. "I almost did. But then you had to go and be all… gracious. And charming. And— ugh."

"Terrible, isn't it?"

"The worst."

I laugh. "You handled it, though."

"Oh, yeah. Nothing screams 'handling it' like insulting half the audience before the event even starts."

"They loved it."

"They did not."

"That one lady basically gave you a standing ovation."

"She publicly endorsed farting husbands."

I wave her off. "She just said she loved *her*husband."

Scarlett doesn't say anything for a second, then downs half her drink like it personally offended her.

I need to change the subject.

"So how's Rip?" she asks, flicking a chip at me. "I assume he's getting the royal treatment now that you're back in town."

"He misses the beach."

"Don't we all."

"He's also mad I took away his freedom to wander into other people's yards."

She gives me a slow, unimpressed blink. "He only liked me for my peanut butter."

"Same."

Her mouth drops open, and I grin.

The navy dress she's wearing hugs her waist and shows just enough leg to make my brain short-circuit. She's a walking contradiction—gorgeous, infuriating, and totally off-limits—and I'm screwed six ways from Sunday because she doesn't even know what she does to me.

"See?" I say, nudging her knee with mine under the table. "You're laughing. Told you this place is magical."

She rolls her eyes, but there's a reluctant smile tugging at her lips. It's the kind of smile she doesn't realize she's giving me. The kind I want to earn again and again.

She taps her straw against the glass. "So. Hockey."

I lift a brow. "You want to talk about hockey?"

"Not particularly. But I know it's your thing."

I shrug. "It's been good. Season kicks off soon. Training starts next week."

"You ready for it?"

"Yeah," I say. Then add, "Sort of."

She catches the hesitation, sharp as ever. "Sort of?"

I shrug again, more careful this time. "There's just… pressure this year. With the captaincy on the table. Contract negotiations. All that."

"You'll get it," she says like it's a fact. "You're good at what you do."

I stare at her for a second too long, thrown off by the simple certainty in her voice.

"Thanks," I say, quieter than I meant to.

She nods, eyes flicking away like she's realizing she said too much.

I don't bring up her book. I don't mention the critic or the pressure she's under. She already looked like the world was sitting on her chest tonight, and I'm not going to add to it.

So instead, I tip my glass toward hers and say,

"To tacos and tequila."

She lifts hers, smirking. "And farting husbands."

"May we never become them."

We clink glasses, and just like that, the tension starts to bleed away.

And even though this wasn't part of the plan—and she'll probably go back to pretending to hate me tomorrow—tonight? It feels like a win.

For both of us.

I'm standing in my kitchen, holding a cup of coffee I haven't actually managed to drink, scrolling through my phone while Rip chews a slipper in the corner like it personally offended him.

The internet has… opinions.

Big ones.

I swipe through post after post, each more unhinged than the last.

> @StampedeFan1: The tension between Chase and Scottie? I want to bottle it. Inject it. Use it as perfume.

> @RomanceLuver34: Enemies to lovers, but make it sports edition. I need this to be real.

> @HockeyRomanceQueen: Not Scar-

lett Calloway going feral over romance novels while sitting next to a literal romance novel cover model in a suit.

@HockeyGossipHQ: He looked at her like she was the final goal in a Game 7 overtime. I can't breathe.

I rub a hand over my face.

There's a side-by-side screenshot of me smirking and her glaring—captioned *"He's thinking about kissing her. She's thinking about committing a crime."*

Rip snorts like he agrees.

I chuckle and blow on my coffee.

I scroll some more, and yeah—it's everywhere. #ChaseAndScottie is trending, and some genius already made a meme comparing us to *Pride and Prejudice*. (I'm Darcy, apparently. I think that's good?)

There's a short video clip from the Q&A where her mic caught her monologue about husbands and how romance novels have never improved anyone's life... followed immediately by a zoomed-in shot of my face trying not to laugh.

I watch it twice.

Okay, three times.

She was mortified last night, and I probably didn't help by taking her out for margaritas and looking at her like she personally ended my dry spell with one snarky comment.

But damn, she was good up there. Even when she was unraveling. Even when she was defensive and awkward and very clearly hating every second of being vulnerable in public.

She held her own.

And the fans loved it. Loved her.

Whether she wants to admit it or not, she just helped take this book club to the next level.

I toss my phone on the counter and finally take a sip of my now lukewarm coffee.

One thing's clear—Scottie Calloway might not believe in love stories, but the rest of the world?

They're already shipping ours.

I set the phone down and make myself focus on breakfast. A spinach omelet for me and a bowl of fresh dog food for Rip.

My phone buzzes across the counter, dancing slightly from the force of the call. I glance at the screen and groan.

Tyler.

I swipe to answer. "Morning, sunshine."

"You alive?" he asks by way of greeting. "Wasn't sure after that PR circus last night."

I laugh, heading for the fridge to put away Rip's food. "Barely. The internet thinks I proposed to her mid-Q&A."

"You kinda looked like you wanted to."

"She looked like she wanted to throat punch

me," I counter.

"Same thing."

I snort. "What's up?"

"You wanna lift? I'm hitting that gym over on Main in twenty. Get your ass out of retirement."

I look down at Rip, who's still gnawing on the slipper like it's his full-time job. "Yeah, alright. Let me drop the kid off at doggy daycare. I'll meet you there."

Forty-five minutes later, we're spotting each other under fluorescent lights in a place that smells aggressively like sweat and testosterone. Tyler, our second-line forward and chaos gremlin of the team, is grinning like he's been waiting to bring this up.

"So… Scottie Calloway, huh?"

I sigh and rack the barbell. "Not happening."

"Shame. You two had more chemistry than that time you tried to make pasta and lit your stove on fire."

"That was *one* time."

"She looked good last night."

This comment strangely makes me want to hit him.

"She always looks good." It slips out without thinking.

Tyler raises a brow. "Damn. That was fast."

"Shut up."

He tosses me a water bottle, smug. "You gonna ask her out?"

"No." I wipe my face with a towel. "She's the exact opposite of my type."

"Which means you like her."

I hate how perceptive this damn dude is.

"She writes books about how men are a scam, Tyler."

"Yeah, but you're a hot scam."

Again, he's not wrong.

I flip him off.

He grins wider. "Tell you what. I bet you can't get her to agree to go on one real date with you before the book club ends."

I stare at him. "What are we, twelve?"

My brain flashes to the tacos and margs we shared last night... But it wasn't a date, and I know Scarlett would set me straight if anyone suspected it was. It was a friendly post-work happy hour. We were maybe slipping into *friend* territory, but I *date* territory was a long ways off.

"C'mon. It's not like you've got anything better to do. You're not serious about her. She hates your guts. You love a challenge." He smirks. "You get her to say yes—without begging or bribing—and I'll pick up your bar tab for the rest of the season."

I pause.

Think of the online chaos. Her glare. The way she practically spit fire into the microphone last night. The way she looked in that dress, legs crossed under the table, lips pouting with that deep red lipstick. Her laughing over tacos. The tiniest crack in her armor.

"I'm not gonna trick her into anything," I say slowly.

Tyler holds up both hands. "She's gotta say yes of her own free will. You gotta actually convince her you're worth it."

I think about it for another second.

Then I nod. "You're on."

Because the truth is—I'm not sure I can. But do I want to try.

18

NOT THAT EASY

Scarlett

My laptop is mocking me. I know I should be working, but I can't bring myself to do it right now.

With a frustrated groan, I minimize the document and lean back in my desk chair. Outside, the Dallas skyline glows faintly through the windows, and my apartment is obnoxiously quiet, which I normally love. But tonight? It feels suffocating.

I should be cranking out words. I have a deadline. I have a contract. I have a platform that's waiting for my next groundbreaking declaration about female independence and why romantic love is a scam perpetuated by Hallmark and Big Chocolate.

But all I can think about is Chase freaking Remington.

And tacos. And tequila. And the fact that for

a guy who annoys the ever-loving hell out of me, he was annoyingly... kind last night. Not to mention stupidly attractive in that dress shirt with his sleeves rolled up, showing forearms doing things I don't want to discuss.

Ugh.

I toss my phone onto the couch across from me to avoid the temptation to text him.

It buzzes.

I stare at it.

It buzzes again.

Okay, *rude*. I cross the room and snatch it up, trying not to feel the ridiculous flutter in my chest when I see his name.

Chase: *So when does the anti-romance merch line drop? I want a hoodie that says "Romance Novels Have Never Helped Anyone" on the back.*

I blink. Then laugh. Then groan because—of course—he's still thinking about that. And of course he couldn't just be a gentleman and let me forget my atrocious hot take.

Me: *Limited edition. Comes with a mug that says "Love is for suckers."*

Chase: *Amazing. I can't wait to wear the full set to my next press conference.*

Me: *Please do. Really lean into your villain era. You never know—it could do wonders for your career.*

There's a pause, and I can almost picture him smirking, thumbs hovering above his phone.

Chase: *Appreciate the career tip lol.*

Me: *How does it feel to be the internet's boyfriend right now?*

Chase: *Is that what's happening?*

I send an emoji of a person shrugging.

Chase: *Real talk. You were good last night. Brave. Just wanted to say that.*

I stare at the screen.
That's... unexpected.
And worse? It makes something twist in my stomach. Something warm. Something terrifying.

Me: *You're not making fun of me?*

Chase: *Not this time. You held your own. Also, I think that lady wanted to be your best friend.*

I bite back a smile.

Me: *I was kind of a disaster.*

Chase: *You were honest. People like that. I liked it.*

Why does he keep doing this?
I should leave it there. Shouldn't reply. Should definitely not indulge this fluttery, stupid feeling in my chest.
But then my thumbs move like they have a mind of their own.

Me: *Thanks. For the tacos, too. (And the margarita the size of my head.)*

Chase: *Anytime, Calloway. Just say the word and I'll bring a barbacoa burrito to your doorstep.*

Somehow, I think he really would. He'd be that kind of boyfriend. A complete golden retriever. A total cinnamon roll… at least in the beginning, cutesy stage. Before the inevitable heartbreak, death, and destruction stage.

Still, I can't help but lean into this a little.

Me: *Tempting. You bribing me with food now?*

Chase: *Would it work?*

Yes.
No.
Maybe.

Ugh.

Me: *Not a chance.*

I toss my phone onto the cushion again and fold my arms, as if that will somehow shut down the heat crawling up my neck.

This is fine. Just casual banter. Post-event debriefing. Nothing to see here.

Nothing at all.

Except the tiniest, most inconvenient thought forming in the back of my mind—

I don't hate talking to him.

And that's probably the most dangerous thing of all.

The little bell above the nail salon door jingles as we step inside, and I'm immediately hit with the scent of lavender, nail polish, and judgment. It's the kind of place with plush pink chairs, cucumber water in glass dispensers, and calming spa music that makes me want to scream.

Harper inhales like she's just arrived in heaven. "Ah. The sacred temple of self-care."

I snort. "It's a pedicure, not a pilgrimage."

She shoves me gently toward the counter. "You're getting the deluxe scrub and the hot stone massage. You need it."

"What I need is a miracle," I mutter under my breath.

We're seated a few minutes later, our feet soaking in warm water, the world blissfully quiet except for the occasional chime of an unsilenced cell phone and the faint sound of Enya in the background.

"You've been quiet," Harper says, eyeing me over the rim of her glass. She's already half-done with her mimosa.

I stare at the bubbles in my foot bath. "I don't know if I can do this."

She blinks. "The pedicure?"

"The book."

Harper sets her glass down, serious now. "Talk to me."

I sigh, dragging a hand through my hair. "It's not coming. I keep trying to write the book I think people expect from me—strong, independent, anti-love—but it feels… hollow. Like I'm just recycling old arguments. Nothing feels honest."

She frowns. "You're putting way too much pressure on yourself."

"I'm under contract. I don't get to take my sweet time and find inspiration while I twirl around in a meadow somewhere. I need words. Now."

Plus, quite frankly, I tried that already. That was the whole idea with the Michigan beach town. It didn't work. If anything, it only confused me further… meeting Chase.

Harper leans back, thoughtful. "What if you stopped trying to write the book they expect from you?"

I glance over. "And do what instead?"

"Write the book you need to write." She shrugs. "Screw the brand. Screw the critics. What do you want to say?"

I open my mouth to answer—and promptly shut it.

Because I have no idea.

That's the most terrifying part.

She studies me for a second, then smirks, just a little. "Also, not to add fuel to the existential crisis, but if you end up falling for the hot hockey player you claim to hate, I'm never letting you live it down."

I narrow my eyes. "That's not happening."

"We'll see," she says breezily, lifting her mimosa again. "Might make a good plot twist, though."

"Can you be for real right now? I'm having a crisis, Harp. And you want to taunt me?"

She leans closer, eyes locked on mine. "I think you've got this," she says, voice softer now. "You're brilliant, Scottie. Even if you can't see it right now."

I don't reply. Just lean back and close my eyes.

Later that night, I'm sitting on my couch in pajamas, laptop balanced on my knees, staring at a blinking cursor and resisting the urge to throw it across the room when my phone rings.

Harper.

I answer on the second ring. "Please tell me you don't already regret that glitter polish."

"You were right," she says, no greeting.

"Wait, what?"

"About the book. About how you feel stuck. I've been thinking about it all afternoon, and I was wrong to push. I gave you bad advice. You don't need to force yourself to fit into anyone's expectations."

I blink. "Are you okay? Is this some sort of early apology for when you inevitably get arrested for trespassing again?"

She laughs. "Shut up. I'm serious. You're the author. You get to tell the story you want to tell. Full stop. Just trust yourself, okay?"

I exhale slowly, the knot in my chest loosening just a fraction. "I wish it were that easy."

"I know," she says. "But maybe start there. Just write what's real. Screw everything else."

I don't answer right away.

Because maybe—just maybe—she's right.

There's a long pause, and then Harper continues. "And… maybe your problem isn't the book. Maybe it's the fact that a certain hockey player has taken up permanent real estate in that grumpy little brain of yours."

"I'm sorry—*what?*" I all but sputter.

"I've seen the way you talk about him," she singsongs. "All that protesting and eye-rolling? Classic denial."

"You're insane."

"I'm just observant. And honestly, if you did fall for him, I'd never let you live it down."

I narrow my eyes. "Is that a bet?"

She laughs. "More like a prophecy. But sure. Let's call it a bet. I say by the end of this book club fiasco, you're going to catch real feelings for Chase Remington."

I snort. "You're delusional."

"Prove me wrong, Calloway. That man could charm the stripes off a zebra."

"I'm not a zebra," I point out. "I'm a cactus. Uncharmable."

She rolls her eyes. "You're insufferable is what you are."

19

PUCK AROUND AND FIND OUT

Scarlett

My phone buzzes with a text from an unknown number, and for once, I'm hoping it's a spam bot trying to sell me discounted yoga pants or tell me I've won a free cruise. Because I don't need any actual disruptions right now. I'm trying to work.

I grab it and glance at the message.

Unknown Number: *Hi! This is Lucy Wilder—I got your number from Vivian (hope that's okay). I used to do the book club thing with the Stampede, and now I'm married to one of the guys (Bennett #88, the hot one with the dimples). Anyway, I wanted to say hi and also—if you're free tomorrow night, I'd love to in-*

*vite you to the home opener. Great
seats, fun crowd, zero pressure.*

I blink at the message. Lucy Wilder.

Okay. Unexpected.

I've seen clips of her online—bright smile, sarcasm for days, somehow managing to hold her own among a team full of hockey players and rabid romance fans. She seemed... terrifyingly cool.

And now she's inviting me to a game?

I should say no. I have nothing to wear. I don't know the rules. The only thing I know about hockey is that Chase plays it, and that's not exactly a glowing endorsement.

Still...

I have nothing else going on tomorrow night. I'm out of peanut butter. And I could use a distraction.

But *hockey* of all things?

I stare at the message a second longer.

I don't do sports.

I don't do crowds.

I *definitely* don't do group bonding events filled with small talk, free T-shirts, and overpriced beer.

But... I also don't have plans tomorrow. Or the next day. Or the day after that, unless you count "ugly cry on the floor in sweatpants and argue with a Google Doc."

I blink at the message, reread it twice, and then check to make sure I haven't hallucinated it entirely. Nope. It's real. I've been invited to a professional hockey game by the unofficial queen of the Stampede WAGs.

I sigh and type back.

> Me: *Hey! That's actually... really nice of you. Sure. Why not? I've never been to a hockey game. (Prepare to answer a thousand dumb questions.)*

> Lucy: *Yay! I'll leave you a pass at will call. Bring a jacket—it gets cold.*

> *And no dumb questions. Just wait. You'll love it.* 😄

The second I step into the arena, I'm hit with the smell of popcorn, the blast of cold air, and the overwhelming hum of thousands of people buzzing with anticipation. The place is *alive*—flashing lights, pounding music, giant faces of sweaty men projected on screens the size of billboards. What in the world? I don't get the hype, but I follow the signs to will call and get my ticket.

The stadium is packed, a sea of jerseys and face paint and the unmistakable smell of soft pretzels and spilled Bud Light. It's chaos. Loud, messy, *absolutely electric* chaos.

Lucy finds me just inside the VIP entrance, wearing a royal blue Stampede jacket over a sparkly tank top, her golden hair pulled into a ponytail that somehow looks casual and glamorous at the same time.

"Scottie!" She grins, pulling me into a hug like we've known each other for years. "You came!"

"Well, you invited me, and I had no excuse," I say, then add, "Unless you count a looming deadline and a lifelong skepticism of organized sports."

Lucy laughs. "You're gonna fit in just fine."

She leads me through a maze of people and security until we're courtside—sorry, *rinkside?*—in plush seats with a perfect view of the ice.

"This is… intense," I say, already looking forward to the start of the game more than I thought I would.

Lucy nods. "You're gonna love it. You'll see."

I find my seat near the glass just as the lights dim and the announcer's voice booms through the speakers like God narrating a Netflix trailer.

"Welcome to opening night, Stampede fans!"

I flinch at the sudden burst of pyrotechnics. The crowd roars. The players skate out through flashing lights and smoke machines like rockstars making a grand entrance—helmets gleaming, jerseys crisp, shoulders squared with oversized protective gear and ridiculous amounts of swagger.

I'm sorry…but what in the world is this?!

And then I see him.

Chase.

He's the last one out. The crowd gets even louder when his name is called.

"Number 91—Chase Remington!"

My stomach flips.

He's in full gear now, and he looks huge. He moves like a weapon—like confidence and precision and brute force all wrapped up in a six-foot-something body that skates like it was born on ice.

Lucy watches me, grinning like she knows exactly what I'm thinking. I smile back, try to play it cool. Sit down. Sip my soda. Tell myself I am here as a journalist of life. An observer of the absurd. A detached, unbiased critic of this weird, out-of-body experience they call hockey.

But ten minutes into the game, I'm… engaged. Like, fully engaged.

Fifteen minutes in, I'm yelling at the refs like they can actually hear me.

By the second period?

I'm banging on the glass and shouting, "OPEN YOUR EYES, REF, HE GOT TRIPPED!" while Lucy cackles beside me.

"Wow," she wheezes, passing me another nacho. "I didn't know you were gonna go full gladiator."

"I didn't either," I pant. "But that was a *flagrant* foul and no one seems to care."

"They never do," she agrees. "Welcome to hockey."

I don't know what's happening to me. I'm standing up half the time. I'm booing like I've been doing it for years. I don't *do* sports. I don't yell. I don't lose composure.

But there I am, completely *uncomposed*, screaming at a grown man on skates like I've got money riding on it.

And watching Chase is… not what I expected at all.

He skates like he was born with blades on his feet.

He's not at all the golden retriever he is in real life. On the ice?

He's… different.

Sharper. Focused. Dangerous, almost.

He crashes into an opposing player, wins the puck, and glides down the ice with all the speed and power of a tsunami.

Lucy elbows me. "Chase looks good tonight."

I don't answer.

Mostly because I'm trying not to ogle him like a thirst trap.

And somehow, as if he *knows*, he looks toward the stands. Not scanning the crowd—looking. Right. At. Me.

His brows raise, the corners of his mouth twitch like he's trying not to laugh.

Because yeah, I'm on my feet.
Banging on the glass.
Screaming like I've lost my mind.
And judging by the glint in his eye?
He's a little scared.
A little amused.
And maybe—a little turned on?

20

HOCKEY ISN'T STUPID (APPARENTLY)

Chase

We won. Barely. But a win's a win.

I tug off my jersey, my muscles still buzzing from the adrenaline rush of the game, and I can't stop thinking about one very specific moment—no, not my goal in the second period, though yeah, that was nice. Not even my hit on Garcia that sent him spinning like a top.

Nope.

The highlight of the night?

Scarlett Calloway—banging on the glass like she was trying to will the puck into the net. Screaming at the refs like she was personally offended by their calls, standing up from her seat, cheering, and absolutely losing her mind when we scored the game-winner in overtime.

I swear, I almost forgot to skate back to the

bench. I was too busy staring.

I didn't expect her to come. I mean, yeah, Lucy said she invited her, but I didn't think she'd actually show up. And if she did, I figured she'd sit quietly in the corner, maybe roll her eyes through the whole thing.

What I got?

A full-throttle, trash-talking, glass-pounding maniac in jeans and a sweater.

I'm a little scared of her. A little impressed. And a whole lot turned on.

"Yo, Remington," Tyler calls from across the room, tossing a roll of tape at me. "Earth to lover boy. You gonna shower or just stand there like you're writing her name in your diary?"

"Shut up," I mutter, catching the tape and chucking it right back at his head.

He laughs and ducks, still grinning like an idiot. "She looked good tonight."

"I didn't notice."

"Sure," he says, heading for the showers. "Tell that to the drool on your chin."

I ignore him and grab a towel, but I'm still thinking about her. She did look good; he's right. Her hair was loose and wavy. And I'm still picturing the flush in her cheeks, the wild energy in her eyes. Like this wasn't just a game to her—it was something she actually cared about.

So the woman who doesn't believe in happy

endings believes in power plays, high-sticking penalties, and yelling at professional athletes like they can hear her from section 102.

And I don't know what that means yet.

But damn, I want to find out.

After, we hit up our usual post-game spot—Manny's, a low-key Mexican place a few blocks from the arena. It's loud, full of neon signs, and always smells like fried heaven.

Dash lounges in the booth across from me, already halfway through his first basket of chips. Tyler drops in next to him, still sweating from the game, and Will plops down beside me with a thud and a groan like the eighty-year-old man he insists he's becoming at twenty-nine.

"Cheers to not blowing that lead in the third," Tyler says, holding up his soda like it's champagne.

"Barely," Dash mutters. "If Chase hadn't remembered how to shoot, we'd be crying into our queso right now."

I smirk and steal a chip. "If I had a dollar for every time I saved your ass—"

"You'd still be an overpaid winger with a bad attitude," Will deadpans.

Laughter rolls around the table.

The energy's good tonight. Easy. Like we're riding the high of a win, even if it was by the skin of our teeth.

But my phone buzzes, and suddenly, the game,

the food, the guys—it all fades a little.

Because the name lighting up my screen?

Scarlett.

I sit up straighter, swipe the notification, and open the message.

Scarlett: *Okay, so maybe hockey's not completely stupid. You guys looked good out there. It's so fast-paced and more exciting than I realized.*

I feel my grin before I can stop it.

Dash catches the look. "You sexting already? Damn, Remington, that was fast even for you."

I ignore him, thumbs moving quickly.

Me: *Tell that to the ref you screamed at in the third. Pretty sure you gave him a complex.*

She types back immediately.

Scarlett: *He DESERVED IT. Worst call I've seen in my life.*

I can't stop smiling like an idiot. I probably look like I just fell in love with my burrito.

"You texting your mom or your soulmate?" Tyler asks, stealing my queso.

"Neither," I say, trying to sound casual. "Just a friend."

"Sure," Will mutters. "The same 'friend' who looked like she wanted to maul you through the glass tonight."

"I think she wanted to maul the ref," I say, taking another bite. "But I wouldn't have minded."

That earns a round of whistles and fake swooning from the table.

"She's got you good," Dash says, shaking his head. "I give it a week before you're writing poetry in the locker room."

I roll my eyes but keep my phone in my lap. Her texts come quickly, her commentary unfiltered, and every time my screen lights up, it's like a shot of adrenaline straight to the chest.

And the thing is—I've had a lot of women flirt with me. A lot of numbers handed over, a lot of dates, a lot of "oh my God, you're Chase Remington" reactions.

But none of them ever banged on the glass and screamed at a ref, then turned around and told me I was obnoxious.

She's different.

And I don't know where this is going yet.

But I know one thing—I'm not ready for the night to end.

> Me: *Hope you didn't pull anything yelling at the refs tonight.*

Scarlett: *I'm just fine, I can assure you.*

At the risk of the guys completely confiscating

my phone, I fire off one last text before pocketing it.

> Me: *Not gonna lie, you were kind of terrifying in the best way.*

After dinner, I head home, but there's still nothing from Scarlett. I wonder if I said something to annoy her—probably.

I take Rip out and check my phone again while he does his business.

Still nothing.

It's fine. I lie to myself.

I push the door open and step into the quiet, dark condo. Rip trots in ahead of me, nails tapping across the hardwood like he owns the place. Which, to be fair, he probably does.

I drop my keys into the dish by the door and kick off my shoes, tugging my hoodie over my head as I head toward the kitchen. The fridge light glows way too bright when I open it, but I ignore it and grab a bottle of water. Rip watches me expectantly like he's waiting for something exciting to happen.

"Sorry, bud," I murmur, twisting the cap off. "No late-night snacks tonight. We're old and responsible now."

He huffs like he doesn't believe me for a second.

I make my way down the hall, and Rip trots

along behind me, already ahead of me in the bedroom, curling up in his usual spot—the bottom left corner of the bed, like clockwork.

I toss the covers back and sink into the mattress, stretching out with a sigh. I'm tired. I should be asleep in minutes.

But my brain has other plans.

I scroll for a second on my phone—checking the usual. Team group chat blowing up about the game. A video someone posted of that power play we nailed in the second period. A meme from Dash that makes me grin and shake my head.

Then a notification. A new text pops up.

Scarlett: *So what, is that normal hockey fan behavior?*

I grin instantly, thumb flying.

Me: *100%. You're basically eligible for season tickets now. Also, impressive trash talk. 'You absolute walking penalty' is a new personal favorite.*

She replies so fast it's like she was waiting for me to say something.

Scarlett: *He elbowed your teammate in the face and didn't even get a whistle. I was morally obligated to say something. Also, don't think I didn't see your little smirk when I screamed "open your eyes, ref!"*

Me: *I plead the fifth. But… you looked good out there, Calloway. If we win the next game, you might have to let me buy you a drink.*

The typing dots bounce for a beat.

Scarlett: *You already bought me a drink—the margarita after book club, remember?*

I lean my head back against the headboard, grinning into the dark like a total idiot. Man, she's fun. Sharp, sarcastic, impossible to ignore.

I stare at her last text for a second too long.

Screw it.

I hit call.

It rings once.

Twice.

"Seriously?" she answers, not even a hello. "You're calling me now?"

Her voice is a little breathless, like I surprised her. Like she didn't expect me to actually do it.

"You said you might let me buy you a drink. Wanted to lock it in before you changed your mind."

She exhales. "That's not how texting works, Remington."

"I don't like rules," I say, slouching deeper into my bed. "Besides, you answered. So either you were curious or you just really needed a new excuse to yell at me."

She doesn't say anything.

I smile. "You had fun tonight."

"I didn't say that."

"You didn't have to."

There's a beat of silence. Then—quietly—she says, "Okay. I had fun."

I close my eyes. Let it sink in.

"I'm glad I went," she adds, almost begrudgingly. "I still think you're cocky as hell, but… it was kind of great seeing you do what you're meant to do."

That one hits me harder than I expect.

"Home?" she asks, somehow knowing.

"Yeah."

"Okay, well…" She trails off. "Don't sprain anything watching game replays tonight."

I huff a laugh. "Try not to yell yourself hoarse watching film breakdowns of my penalty kill."

She clicks her tongue. "No promises."

I don't want to hang up.

But I also don't want to tug too hard at whatever fragile thing is building between us.

"Night, Scarlett."

Pause. "Night, Chase."

I set my phone down and stare at the ceiling.

She's still a pain in the ass. Still sarcastic, sharp, and way too sure of herself.

But somehow, that's become one of my favorite things about her.

I turn over and place one hand on Rip's back as he lets out a sleepy sigh.

"I'm screwed, huh?" I mutter.

Rip doesn't answer—just shifts a little closer.

I close my eyes and let the silence take over.

And for the first time in a while, falling asleep doesn't feel so hard.

21

QUESO MAKES EVERYTHING BETTER

Scarlett

My morning starts with an unexpected text.

Lucy Wilder has invited me out.

I thought it over and replied with a snarky text.

> Me: *Fine, but if you try to braid my hair or talk about babies, I'm ghosting you.*

She laughed and told me we'd get along just fine.

Just after seven o'clock, I'm walking into a downtown rooftop bar with string lights overhead and a skyline view.

Lucy stands, gives me a once-over, and grins. "You clean up nice, Calloway." She slides a margarita across the table.

"You sound surprised," I say, taking the drink

and sipping it. "Is this a recruitment dinner? Do I get a WAG initiation badge?"

She laughs. "Please. We're way past branding. This is just a drink between two women who, for better or worse, are now part of the Stampede circus."

I raise a brow. "Better or worse? That doesn't sound very wifey of you."

We sit down across from each other, a basket of chips between us. "Oh, I adore Bennett," she says easily. "But let's not pretend the hockey world isn't its own brand of unhinged."

We clink glasses.

The next hour is… easy. And surprisingly real.

Lucy isn't what I expected. I thought I'd meet another picture-perfect, filtered-to-oblivion Instagram wife. But Lucy is sharp, witty, and unapologetic. She tells me about the early days—working as a paramedic, then accidentally becoming a podcasting powerhouse. She rolls her eyes at internet trolls, talks about advocating for women in sports, and casually mentions dragging an NHL reporter on Twitter once for calling her a distraction.

"I'm not a distraction," she says, sipping her drink. "I'm the reason half his teammates found a damn audience."

I snort into my glass. "You're terrifying. In the best way."

"And you're not?" she says, arching a brow.

"You basically built a career telling women to light their exes on fire and invest in themselves."

"Well, not *literally*," I mutter. "But yeah. Close."

We talk about the book club, about the team, about Bennett.

It's easy from the start—her energy is electric in the best way. She's whip-smart, cutting, and hilarious, and I get the sense that if anyone ever came for her, she'd not only destroy them but also write a witty takedown to publish in *The Atlantic* afterward.

"Okay," I say halfway through margarita number two. "I have to ask."

She raises a brow. "Uh-oh."

"How did *you* fall for a hockey player?"

She grins, but it's a little softer now, thoughtful. "Honestly? I didn't. Not at first."

Okay, this is going to be interesting…

Lucy laughs, remembering some faraway memory. "Bennett is…" She shakes her head, nostalgic and a little annoyed. "He just kept showing up. Not in a creepy way. In a way that made it harder and harder to pretend I didn't want him to."

I pause, absorbing that. "So he wore you down."

"He made me feel seen," she corrects. "He let me be loud and complicated and passionate without ever trying to shrink me. And more than that— he didn't try to convince me that love was perfect.

He just… showed me that the right kind is worth the mess."

I blink.

"Oh no," she says, mock horror crossing her face. "Did I just make you feel something?"

"Disgust," I deadpan. "Mostly that."

She sips her drink and eyes me over the rim. "What's going on with you and Chase?"

"Nothing," I say too quickly.

"Mhm."

"I mean it. He's—he's charming and smug and ridiculous. And yes, he looks unfairly good in a suit, and no, I'm not talking about this."

Lucy grins. "Okay. We don't have to talk about it."

"I hate you."

"No, you don't."

We fall into comfortable banter again, and somewhere between chips and guac and a third margarita, I forget to be on guard. I forget to hold my opinions like weapons. I'm just… me.

It's freeing.

And eventually—the conversation comes back to Chase.

"He drives me insane," I confess. "In a very infuriating, occasionally confusing way."

She smirks. "Welcome to the club. I once threw a donut at Bennett's head during an argument."

"Did it hit him?"

"Frosted side down," she says proudly. "Left a smear on his shoulder. He wore it like a badge of honor."

I laugh harder than I have in weeks. And suddenly, I realize I've been holding tension in my chest for *so long* that I forgot what it feels like to breathe freely.

And even though I made a big production of not wanting to talk about Chase, I can't help the way my brain keeps returning to him. The way he looked on the ice—so powerful and in command. The way he teased me over the phone. I even find myself wondering about Rip.

Lucy leans back in her chair, studying me. "Can I say something kind of cheesy?"

"Do I have a choice?"

She grins. "Nope. You're the real deal, Scarlett. Your work matters. The way you make women feel like they're enough on their own? That's powerful as hell. But—" Her eyes soften. "—it's also okay to be *enough* and still want more. To want softness, intimacy, love."

I go still.

Something in me—something stubborn and deeply buried—shifts.

She doesn't say it like a warning. She says it like a truth. And weirdly, it doesn't feel like an attack on everything I've built. It feels… possible.

And then she says, quieter now, "You know,

your books? It's great the way you make women feel strong and self-sufficient—it's powerful."

I nod, uneasy.

"But," she adds gently, "being strong doesn't mean shutting everyone out. And independence isn't the same thing as loneliness."

I stiffen. "I'm not lonely."

"I didn't say you were." She smiles, not unkind. "But it's okay to want more. It doesn't make you weak. It makes you *human*."

I don't respond right away. My throat's tight, and I don't know why. Maybe because it's been a long time since someone said that to me without pity or a punchline. Just truth. Or maybe it's because I've had too much tequila.

"You're annoying," I say, my voice rough.

Lucy just laughs. "You'll get used to it."

And oddly enough… I kind of hope I do.

We order two baskets of brisket nachos.

And for the first time in a long time, I don't feel like I have to armor up around another woman. I just feel seen.

Understood.

Empowered.

And maybe a little braver than I was an hour ago.

22

CHEMISTRY, BUT MAKE IT COMPETI-TIVE

Chase

I step into the event space and am immediately hit with a wall of perfume, shrieking laughter, and the scent of catered cupcakes. Someone spots me—then someone else—and suddenly I'm surrounded by women waving copies of *The Penalty Box* and asking if Rip is single.

"Unfortunately, he's very taken," I say with a grin, signing a book.

One of them giggles. "Not you. The dog."

Another woman shouts, "Team Scottie forever!"

And just like that, my eyes start scanning for her.

I find Scarlett across the room, perched casually on a high stool near the stage, her legs crossed and her face half-buried in a cup of coffee. She's wearing a silky wine-colored blouse that makes her look like she just stepped off the cover of a fashion magazine—if the fashion magazine was titled *Don't Even Try Me.*

My heart does this dumb little stutter.

I shouldn't be this into her, especially when she's made it abundantly clear that this—whatever it is between us—is just temporary tension. PR and proximity.

But I am. Fully, recklessly, completely into her.

She glances up and catches me looking.

Raises one brow like she's just waiting for me to say something ridiculous.

Challenge accepted.

I weave through the crowd and slide onto the empty stool beside her. "What is that shirt you're wearing? It's very…"

"Very what?" she snaps.

"Distracting."

She doesn't even flinch. "What, like I got dressed specifically to give you a stroke?"

I smirk. "Mission accomplished."

Vivian appears on stage with her clipboard, all business. "Tonight's discussion is themed 'Battle of the Sexes.' We'll be looking at how male and female characters are portrayed in romance—flaws, strengths, double standards… This should be fun."

Scarlett lets out a noise that's somewhere between a laugh and a groan. "This is going to be a bloodbath."

I grin. "You're just mad because you already know you're gonna lose."

"Lose what? You think the average man in a romance novel could survive a single chapter of a book written by me?"

I laugh. "That's exactly what I'm afraid of."

The crowd's already buzzing, everyone taking their seats, phones out and filming. The energy is high, chaotic, and honestly? I'm kind of loving it—much more than I thought I would. I can guess why...

Vivian gestures for us to come up to the front. I stand, offer Scarlett a hand, and she gives me a look like I just offered her a seat on the Titanic.

Still, she takes it.

We sit on the stage, the lights hot, the eyes of a hundred romance readers burning into us.

"Alright," Vivian says. "Let's kick this off. What's the biggest difference between how men and women are written in love stories?"

Scarlett leans toward her mic, all confidence and control. "Men in romance novels are fantasy. Real men would never say half the things these characters say—unless they're trying to get slapped or sued."

There's laughter. She barely hides a smile.

I take my turn. "Women in romance novels are way too skeptical. Like, 'Oh, he brought me soup when I was sick, but what does it mean?' It means he brought you soup, babe."

The audience cracks up.

Scarlett glares at me.

"I'm just saying, sometimes it's not that deep."

"Oh, because men are famously simple creatures. Got it."

I glance at the crowd. "She's proving my point."

More laughter.

The banter goes back and forth—she roasts my taste in books, I tease her about her tragic inability to flirt without sounding like she's about to sue someone.

But underneath the jokes, there's a current. A pull.

And for a second, I wonder if she feels it too.

Because when she laughs—actually laughs at something I say—it hits me square in the chest.

I want to make her laugh again.

And again.

But for now?

I'll take one more hour on this stage where it feels like it's just her and me. The crowd of people fades away, and Scarlett is all I can focus on.

After the event wraps and the crowd starts to thin out, I find her near the refreshment table, swirling what's left of her lemonade like she's thinking very hard about whether or not to throw it at me.

I lean against the table beside her. "You survived."

She sighs. "Barely."

"You crushed it. They loved you."

Her lips twitch. "They loved watching us verbally spar."

"Same thing."

She rolls her eyes but doesn't walk away. Progress. "This isn't a game, you know. There are no winners here."

I grin. "I don't *need* to win." I lift a cup of lemonade and take a slow sip. "I just *like* to."

"I hung out with Lucy the other day," she says casually, like it's not a bomb she's just dropped into the conversation.

I almost choke. "Oh, I've gotta know… what was that like?"

"Basically world domination."

I nod solemnly. "Okay, so pretty much exactly how I pictured it."

She laughs—an actual, unguarded laugh that curls in my chest and settles somewhere I probably shouldn't examine too closely.

We linger there for a beat longer than necessary. Then someone calls her name from across the room, and the spell breaks.

She gives me a nod. "Goodnight, Remington."

"Night, Calloway."

And just like that, she's gone.

Later that night, I'm sprawled in bed, one arm behind my head, the other scrolling my phone while Rip snores dramatically at the foot of the bed like he's had a long day of *doing absolutely nothing.*

My feed?

Absolutely flooded.

@ReaderGirl2000: If enemies-to-lovers isn't real, explain Chase and Scottie.

@BookTokBabe: THE CHEMISTRY. THE BANTER. THE TENSION. I NEED THEM TO KISS IMMEDIATE-LY.

@RomanceRiot: Watching Scottie Calloway slowly realize she might have a crush is like watching a lion accidentally cuddle a golden retriever. I am LIVING.

I scroll through meme after meme. One is a freeze-frame of Scarlett glaring at me mid-panel, captioned: "She wants to hate him so bad, but his biceps are distracting."

Another has both of us side-by-side with "Love is War: Live Edition" splashed across the bottom.

I laugh, open up a text to Scarlett, and type:

Me: *We're trending again. The internet thinks you're in love with me.*

The typing bubbles appear, then disappear. Then reappear. Then finally her message comes through.

Scarlett: *Tell the internet to take several seats.*

Me: *You sure? I think they've got a point.*

Scarlett: *Your ego is terrifying.*

Me: *And yet, you can't look away.*

No reply.

I grin at the screen, toss the phone on my nightstand, and scratch Rip behind the ears.

"Admit it," I murmur. "She likes me."

Rip groans and flops onto his back, unimpressed.

"Fine. Too soon."

But still, I fall asleep smiling.

23

THIS WON'T HURT A BIT

Scarlett

My phone is possessed.

It starts buzzing before the sun is even up, vibrating across the nightstand with the fury of a thousand rabid romance fans. I bury my head under the pillow and groan. Maybe if I ignore it long enough, the notifications will give up and go haunt someone else.

Spoiler: they don't.

Eventually, the buzzing gets so aggressive it knocks a lip balm onto the floor.

I sit up with a dramatic sigh and squint at the screen.

Ninety-seven unread messages.

Why?

I swipe through them with bleary eyes. Texts from Harper, Lucy, my editor, and even my brother, who hasn't read a book since *The Very Hungry Caterpillar*, has somehow joined the party.

Harper: *WTF DID YOU DO?*

YOU'RE TRENDING

YOU AND HOT HOCKEY GUY = IN-TERNET MELTDOWN

Lucy: *Hey, ignore the chaos. You were brilliant. Also, Bennett says if you don't marry Chase, he's personally going to adopt him.*

Okay, that was a weird comment. I keep reading. The next message is from my editor.

Tabitha: **Whatever you're doing, KEEP DOING IT. Also, it would be great if you could ride this wave into a new draft?? :) **

I groan and toss the phone on the bed like it's personally betrayed me.

Because of course. Of course the entire internet has lost its collective mind over one harmless (okay, slightly chaotic) book club debate.

I open social media next. *Big mistake.*

There's a fan cam of Chase smirking at me while I'm mid-rant. Someone captioned it: "He looks like he's already picked out their honeymoon destination."

Another one:

"I didn't believe in enemies to lovers until this moment. I would die for this tension."

And the cherry on top?

A poll:

"Do you think Scottie Calloway will cave and go on a date with Chase Remington?"
The current vote?

96% YES.

I stare at the screen. Hard.

Then I close the app and let my head thunk back against the pillow.

I am never leaving my apartment again.

Ever.

A minute later, a new message pings.

Chase: *You okay?*

My thumbs get to work immediately, and since I'm so worked up, I have to retype my message three times to avoid any typos.

Scarlett: *Absolutely not.*

Chase: *The fans are unhinged. But I kinda love it.*

I roll my eyes so hard I see my childhood.

Me: *Of course you do.*

You thrive on chaos.

Chase: *You say that like it's a bad thing.*

Also, you looked good last night

Like, really good.

Just saying.

I toss the phone aside again before my brain short-circuits. Because I'm not doing this. I'm not engaging. I'm not going to smile at my screen like a giddy idiot because a hockey player who drives me insane says I looked good.

(Okay, fine. I *do* smile. But it's small. Barely counts.)

I push the blankets off and drag myself to the kitchen, trying to remind myself that I am a grown woman with a career and a backbone—not someone who gets flustered over banter and a stupidly charming smile.

I open the fridge. Nothing but oat milk and half a lime.

Perfect.

Maybe I'll go for a workout. Clear my head. Avoid the internet.

And definitely *not* text Chase back.

Probably.

Maybe...

Ugh.

The house is gorgeous, of course. One of those airy modern builds with oversized furniture, giant windows, and enough throw pillows to smother a grown man. It smells like a candle store and success.

Lucy nudges me inside with a grin. "You're going to love them. They're chaos in the best way."

"I don't do well with groups," I murmur under my breath.

I'm still not sure why I agreed to this, but when Lucy suggested a girls' night out, I said yes. I'd had so much fun with her—both at the hockey game and when we went out for margaritas—but now?

Now I'm regretting saying yes.

She rolls her eyes. "Please. You've survived book club meetings. This'll be cake."

We walk through the open-concept kitchen and into the living room, where a handful of the Stampede wives and girlfriends—WAGs, apparently, which sounds like a golden retriever convention—are already gathered around a charcuterie board the size of a sled.

The wine is flowing. The laughter is loud.

Lily—wife of the goalie—Lucy whispers to me, is mid-story. "—and then I walk into the kitchen, and my husband is trying to fix the garbage disposal with a hockey stick. Like, *as a tool.* Just jamming it in there like it was Excalibur."

The group erupts in laughter.

"Wait, did it work?" someone asks.

"No! He broke the stick and somehow made the disposal even more jammed. We had to call a plumber *and* the team equipment guy."

Lucy lifts her glass. "To hockey husbands— beautiful idiots, the lot of them."

"Hear, hear," someone chimes.

Lily grins at me. "Your turn, Scarlett. Got any horror stories?"

"Oh, I'm not married," I say. "Or dating a hockey player. Or anyone. I'm the token emotionally detached feminist here tonight."

Lucy winks. "That's why we like you."

A brunette in leggings pipes up. "Okay, but listen to this. My husband tried to name our dog *Zamboni.*"

Collective groans from around the room.

She continues, nodding. "And I said no, but he literally started calling it that anyway. Now the dog ignores me unless I use that name."

I nearly spit out my wine. "A fluffy traitor!"

"Exactly," she groans.

"I have one," Lucy says, already giggling. "So

Bennett made me a smoothie last week and accidentally used pre-workout instead of protein powder. I was just trying to have a chill morning yoga session, but instead, I blacked out and reorganized our spice rack by pH level."

We lose it.

"And don't even get me started on game-day superstitions," another girl says, shaking her head. "Six alarms. Starting at 4:36 a.m. Two minutes apart. Every game day. I now know true psychological warfare. And it comes in the form of iPhone ringtones."

"Okay, but points for creativity," Lucy says.

Harper would love this, I think. I can practically hear her saying *See? These women didn't give up their whole identity. They're still brilliant and independent... just also in love.*

"I've said it before," another woman says, reaching for a cracker, "but I'll say it again: they may be elite athletes, but they're also one bad day away from eating cereal for dinner out of a measuring cup."

The group erupts into laughter, and Lucy leads me to the couch with a glass of white wine already in hand.

"Everyone, this is Scarlett," she announces. "Author. Book club co-host. Tolerates Chase Remington on a semi-regular basis."

There's a chorus of oohs and "God help you,"

followed by a spot being made for me on the couch between two of the women, who immediately offer me cheese and emotional support.

Okay, so maybe tonight won't be so bad after all.

A dark-haired girl who is going *hard* on the prosecco turns to me. "I honestly love your books, by the way."

"Oh?" I blink, caught off guard.

"Yeah," says a blonde with a sharp bob. "It's refreshing to hear someone say you don't need to lose yourself in a relationship. I got married young, and it took me years to realize I was allowed to still have opinions."

"You're the one who writes those empowerment books, right?" the brunette next to me asks. "The 'you don't need a man' manifesto?"

I blink. "That's… probably an oversimplification, but yeah."

Her eyes go wide. "I *love* that. Honestly. I wish I had that mindset before I got married."

More laughter. More wine.

And then suddenly we're all just talking. About relationships. About expectations. About how hard it is to hold onto yourself when your life gets tied to someone else's schedule, career, or spotlight.

"You're kind of living the dream," one woman says. "Like, don't get me wrong, I love my guy. But the freedom? The peace of not dealing with dirty socks on the floor? Don't let anyone make you give that up."

"Seriously," another chimes in. "The independence thing? That's hot. Don't let some guy make you think you have to soften it."

I take a sip of my wine, feeling oddly warm— not just from the alcohol, but from the unexpected camaraderie.

"I won't," I say, smiling faintly. "Trust me. I've worked too hard to get here."

Lucy clinks her glass to mine. "Damn right you have."

We settle into the couch, laughter echoing around the room, the soft hum of a playlist underscoring the conversations. And for once, I don't feel like the odd woman out. I feel… understood.

It's disarming.

I'm having more fun than I expected. I thought these women might be stuck up or worse—judgmental. But they're neither.

And they're sharing all the tea about what it's like to have a hockey husband. Possible ammo to hang over Chase's head someday…

I'm here for it.

24
THE GUT PUNCH

Scarlett

I'm halfway through my workout, earbuds in, trying to drown out the internet noise with a podcast about finding peace in chaos—which is ironic, considering I am the chaos at the moment.

The gym is surprisingly empty at this time of morning, and I'm already fifteen minutes in, according to the treadmill, which *should* feel like a great start. But I'm still spiraling. When I need grounding, I do what any self-respecting masochist would

do: I open Instagram.

Harper always says I'm asking for it. And she's right.

I scroll aimlessly for a minute, pausing on a few dog videos, liking a new release announcement from one of my author friends, and then—

I see *his* name.

A smiling couple. Champagne flutes raised. A golden hour photo filtered within an inch of its life. The woman is pretty in that Pinterest board way—flowy hair, pastel dress, the kind of effortless that takes three hours and a glam team.

And him.

My ex.

The one I loved so hard I nearly lost myself.

The one who told me I was selfish for choosing my career.

The one who made me feel like I'd never be enough.

Now? He's smiling for the camera, arm wrapped around someone new, and the caption reads:

"Engaged to my best friend. May can't come fast enough."

My breath catches.

There it is. The gut punch I didn't know I was waiting for.

I stop walking.

The podcast keeps playing—something about being present and letting go—but the words blur behind the buzzing in my ears.

He's getting married.

He's moving on, promising someone else the forever he swore to me, then yanked away when I dared to have dreams of my own.

My fingers tighten around my phone.

It shouldn't bother me. Not after all this time. Not after everything I've built.

But it does.

And I *hate* that it does.

I blink hard and stuff my phone into my pocket, jaw clenched. This is why I don't do love stories. This is why I don't believe in happy endings.

This right here.

And yet, a new thought pushes in—uninvited, unwelcome.

If he could fall in love again... could I?

Nope.

I hop off the treadmill and head home, ignoring the sting in my chest and the tightness in my throat.

Because I don't want love.

I want a deadline extension, a decent cup of coffee, and the world to stop asking me to feel things.

That's it.

By the time I get back to the house, my head is still spinning. I don't even remember the drive— just flashes of traffic lights and the uncomfortable silence.

I peel off my leggings in the hallway, strip off my top on the way to the bathroom, and turn the water on too hot. Just to feel something.

Thirty minutes later, I'm freshly scrubbed, swaddled in an oversized robe, and have my wet hair wrapped in a towel like a turban. I walk straight to the bed, ignore the pile of laundry I meant to do two days ago, and fling myself across it.

Then I grab my phone and text Harper.

Me: *You up?*

Harper: *Always. Spill it.*

Me: *I'm coming over. I'm bringing wine. And I'm emotionally unstable.*

That last part kind of goes without saying; it's barely after 11 a.m.

Ten minutes later, I'm at her door.

She answers in fuzzy socks and a tank top that says *Main Character Energy*. Honestly, it's a vibe.

"I brought the good cab," I say, holding up the bottle.

"Bless you. Come in. Do you want snacks or just a crash mat and a friend-slash-therapist?"

"Both," I sigh, dropping onto her couch as if the weight of my feelings is physically too much to carry.

Harper returns with two glasses and a bowl of popcorn so aggressively buttered it could be illegal in some states. She hands me a glass, flops down beside me, and gives me The Look.

"Well?"

I press the glass to my forehead. "Graham is getting married."

Her mouth falls open. "Graham... as in *the*

Graham?"

"Do I have another emotionally scarring Graham in my past that I forgot to tell you about?"

She groans and slumps backward into the couch cushions. "Tell me everything. No—wait. Don't. Actually, yes, do."

I hold up my phone and open the Instagram post again. It's still there, bright and shiny and smug. *Can't wait to marry my best friend.* The ring, the sunset, the stupid matching smiles.

And the thing is—he looks good. Like, *good* good. And happy. And I guess I hate that.

Mature of me, I know.

I don't hate it for him.

I hate it for me.

Harper reads it and makes a noise as if she's being personally attacked. "He wears pink now? That is NOT his aesthetic."

"Right?" I throw my arm dramatically across my face. "He looks like an extra in a Hallmark movie."

"Well," she says, sipping her wine, "if you're the one who got away, she's definitely the one who got... suckered?"

I laugh, just once—a weak little sound that gets stuck in my throat.

"I don't know why it hit me so hard," I say after a beat. "I don't want him. I haven't wanted him in forever. We broke up three years ago. But seeing that post just—ugh. It felt like someone punched me."

Harper nods. "Yeah, it's not about *him*. It's about what it stirred up."

"Exactly." I take a long sip of wine. "What if it wasn't just him? What if I'm the problem? What if I don't know how to do any of this, and I've just spent the last few years convincing myself I didn't want it because I was too afraid to try again?"

Harper sets her glass down and gives me a long, unreadable look. "Scarlett…"

I look at her. "Don't say it."

"I'm gonna say it."

"Harper—"

"You're scared."

I groan. "I hate you."

She just smiles and hands me a tissue. "No, you don't."

I sniff. "Maybe a little."

"I'll take it. Now drink your wine and cry it out. You're allowed to have a meltdown, okay? Just don't forget who the hell you are when it's over."

I nod. "Thanks."

I sip my wine and ponder Harper's words.

At its core, I know this isn't about Graham.

It's about *me*.

Something is happening in my life. Maybe it's finally time to deal with my parents' divorce in ways I've avoided all these years. To confront how scary it feels when everything you thought you knew is yanked away, or how to accept that other people can let us down and hurt us when we get too close.

But that worry is for future Scarlett, in a future therapy session.

This Scarlett just wants to complain about her ex and drink wine with her bestie—which is its own kind of therapy.

"Next time," she says, standing up, "you need to give me more warning when we're going to day-drink. I hardly have any snacks."

I let out a weak laugh. "Deal."

Later that evening, I've sobered up and am back home—sitting on my couch, wrapped in a blanket like a sad little burrito—when my phone buzzes.

I let out a sigh and ignore it. I'm mid-meltdown, which is not exactly the vibe I want to share with the world right now.

Something shifted in me today. Between the cabernet and the girl talk, the Chinese takeout and the dinnertime nap… I'm a bit of a mess. I'm dehydrated, for one.

But the screen lights up again, and this time, I see the name.

Chase Remington.

I groan.

The last thing I need is Mr. Sunshine checking in to see how I'm doing when I'm seconds away from drowning in self-pity and the leftover Chinese food I brought home from Harper's.

But my traitorous thumb opens the message anyway.

Chase: *Hey. Just checking in. You good?*

I stare at it for a second.
He doesn't know. He can't know.
Right?
Still, I type back before I can overthink it.

Me: *All good. Just catching up on work stuff.*

Lie. Total lie. The only thing I've accomplished today is discovering that the man who once told me I was his entire future is now marrying someone who probably owns matching kitchen towels and says things like "we're just so aligned spiritually."

His response comes a beat later.

Chase: *Cool. Just felt like you might need someone to remind you you're a badass.*

My chest tightens unexpectedly.
Then another message pops up.

Chase: *And also—I have ice cream. If that helps.*

I stare at the screen, torn between smiling and crying.

Me: *What kind?*

Chase: *Chocolate peanut butter cup. I don't play around.*

I sniff, pulling the blanket down to free my arms.

Me: *Tempting.*

Chase: *I can leave it on your doorstep like a snack fairy. No pressure.*

I glance at the clock. It's late. I look down at my yoga pants and T-shirt-clad body and my general state of emotional disarray.

But the idea of sitting here alone, wallowing, when I could be doing something as simple and silly as eating ice cream with someone who makes me forget—for five minutes—that I'm a mess?

It's more tempting than I want to admit.

Me: *Okay. Five minutes. No pep talks. Just ice cream.*

Chase: *Scout's honor.*

Pause.

Chase: *Unless you were never a Scout.
In which case I'll just promise not to
be annoying.*

Me: *You're always annoying.*

Chase: *Be there in ten.*

I stare at the message for a moment, then toss my phone onto the bed and mutter, "This better be some damn good ice cream."

But underneath

it all? A whisper of relief. A little softness breaking through.

Because even if he doesn't know what's going on, he still thought to check.

And I'm not sure what to do with that.

Ten minutes later, I hear a knock at my door and freeze.

I glance down at my outfit—an oversized T-shirt, yoga pants, and my long hair twisted into a sad excuse for a bun. The emotional devastation look is really working for me tonight.

Another knock. "Scarlett?"

I sigh and get up to answer it.

Chase stands there in joggers and a hoodie, wearing a grin that shouldn't be allowed on some-one this aggravating. In one hand, he holds a pint of ice cream; in the other, Rip is leashed and panting happily, as if he's been summoned for an official emotional support mission.

"Hey," he says, like this is the most normal thing in the world.

Rip pushes past him immediately, sniffs at my feet, and then flops down dramatically across my doormat, his tail thumping.

I blink. "You brought Rip?"

"He's basically a certified comfort professional. He accepts payment in peanut butter and belly rubs."

Rip rolls over onto his back, as if he heard the terms of the agreement and is ready to collect.

I huff a tiny laugh and step aside to let them in.

Thankfully, Chase says nothing about my appearance. I basically look like heartbreak and emotional damage had a baby.

He just hands me the pint and a spoon, then drops onto my couch like he's been here before. I remain standing for a moment, watching Rip trot into my living room like he owns the place, before I finally sit down too.

Rip immediately climbs into my lap.

Correction: he *attempts* to climb into my lap. It's more of a large-dog flop that results in me half-straddled under eighty pounds of fluffy fur. My knees are numb, but my heart feels surprisingly lighter.

Chase looks far too pleased with himself. "Told you. Therapy dog."

I stroke a hand down Rip's side, my fingers sinking into his thick fur. "Okay, yeah, this is working suspiciously well."

He shrugs and opens his own pint. "He's good at his job."

I dig into the chocolate peanut butter cup, letting the cold sweetness anchor me.

We sit in silence for a moment. Rip lays his head on my belly and blinks up at me with his big brown eyes.

Chase leans back, his arm draped along the back of the couch—close but not touching. "Wanna tell me what happened?"

I shake my head. "Not really."

He nods, like that's okay too.

We sit in silence for a beat. Then I say it quietly. "He's getting married."

Chase doesn't ask who. He doesn't press. He just waits.

"My ex," I add, feeling the need to clarify. "The guy I thought was the one. Back when I still believed in all that stuff."

Chase stays quiet. I'm sure he's piecing it all together right now.

I gesture with my spoon. "Instagram announcement. Filtered to hell. They look like a stock photo. 'When you know, you know,' she wrote in the caption." I scoff. "I knew too. At least, I thought I did."

Chase leans forward, elbows on his knees, his gaze steady. "You didn't deserve that."

"I let him in. I let him see all of me. And he still left."

Chase's jaw tightens. "Then he's an idiot."

I blink at him. "What?"

"You let someone in, and they bail? That's not on you, Scarlett. That's on them. He didn't leave because you weren't enough; he left because he wasn't."

I look down at Rip, his head heavy on my lap, and suddenly I want to cry again—but I don't. Because somehow this—ice cream, dog fur, and Chase telling me I'm not unlovable—is doing something dangerous to my chest.

He clears his throat, as if he feels it too. "Also, for the record, chocolate peanut butter cup is a criminally underrated flavor."

I smirk, wiping a tear off my cheek. "You brought it just to say that, didn't you?"

"Partially. Also, because it fixes almost everything."

"And Rip?"

He leans back and props his feet up on my coffee table. "He's here to seal the deal."

Rip lets out a loud snore.

And for the first time today, I laugh—really laugh.

It doesn't fix everything.

But it's a start.

"Can I tell you a secret?" he asks, his eyes filled with that boyish charm I'm not even going to pretend I'm immune to.

I nod.

"You're going to be okay, Scarlett." He says it with complete sincerity, absolute certainty, and not a hint of amusement.

My throat tightens. I take another spoonful of ice cream to keep myself from saying something ridiculous, like thank you or please stay.

But I'm not sure Chase is right. My entire truth has been cemented in the reality that I don't need a man, thank you very much.

Except... I don't believe it anymore.

Not entirely.

And that is the terrifying part.

25

FORMAL WEAR & FLIRTING

Chase

The moment I step into the ballroom, I remember why I hate these things.

Stiff suits. Awkward mingling. Everyone trying to act casual while simultaneously seeking attention.

I tug at the collar of my tux—custom-tailored, yet it still feels like a noose—and scan the room for familiar faces.

Tyler spots me first, raising his glass. "There he is. Looking like James Bond with a penalty record."

I flash him a grin. "Try not to swoon."

My other teammates are scattered throughout the crowd—shaking hands, laughing too loudly, and being charming enough to meet their PR quotas for the night. Just as I'm about to join them, I see her.

Scarlett.

And just like that, I forget how to breathe.

She's across the room, standing near a tall floral arrangement, looking spectacular. Her deep emerald green dress is silky and fitted in all the right ways, hugging her curves like it was custom-made just to torment me. Her hair is swept up, with a few loose strands curling at her neck, and her lipstick is a shade I want to memorize with my mouth.

She hasn't seen me yet.

Which is good, because I need a moment to remember how legs work.

I knew from Vivian that she had been invited to this year's charity gala—but she had been noncommittal when I asked if she planned to attend.

Classic Scarlett to be noncommittal. But I'm really glad she came. I haven't seen her since she was wallowing on her couch with Rip and a pint of ice cream.

"Is that—?" Tyler sidles up next to me and lets out a low whistle. "Damn. She cleans up nice."

I grunt.

"Oh no," he says, clearly enjoying this. "You're a goner."

"Shut up," I mutter.

"She hasn't even looked at you, and you're already undressing her with your eyes. This bet is over before it even started."

I elbow him hard. "It's *not* about the bet."

"Sure it's not. And I'm upping the ante. Forget one date… I bet you can't make her fall for you."

I ignore him and head to the bar, needing something to hold in my hands before I do something stupid, like walk up to her and beg her to dance.

The bartender slides two flutes of champagne across the counter before I even order. Perfect.

When I turn back around, she's closer, laughing at something Harper said, one hand resting lightly on her hip.

She looks radiant. Effortless. Dangerous.

I walk up, heart thudding like I've just finished a third-period shift, and offer her one of the flutes.

She turns at the last second, surprised to see me.

And I swear—her eyes widen just a fraction, as if she feels it too.

I hold out the glass. "For the most stunning woman in the room."

She raises a brow, clearly unimpressed. "I think you meant to find the woman in the red dress. She's been posing for photos by the donation wall all night."

"Nope," I say, stepping just close enough to smell her perfume—something soft and floral that does strange things to my brain. "Got the right one."

A pause.

Then she takes the drink. "You clean up okay, Remington."

I grin. "You make a guy forget how to walk."

"Try not to trip and fall in love. That would be embarrassing."

Too late.

I don't say it. I just raise my glass to hers and try not to stare at her mouth when she takes a sip.

This night just got a lot more interesting.

Her lips twitch as she crosses her arms, glancing sideways at me. "Didn't think black-tie galas were your scene."

"They're not." I take a sip of my champagne. "But I heard a certain bestselling author might be here, and I couldn't resist."

She eyes her champagne, then me. "You showed up here just to annoy me?"

"Partly." I clink my glass against hers. "Also, I look damn good in a tux, and it felt like a waste not to share that with the world."

Her gaze drags slowly down my suit and back up, unimpressed. "You ironed. Congratulations."

"You say that like it's not one of my best qualities."

"Your ego is one of your best qualities."

I grin. "Weird way to say you missed me."

She rolls her eyes but sips the champagne anyway. I take that as a win.

"Should we take a look at the auction items?" I

ask, tipping my chin toward the tables in the back of the room.

"Sure."

The long tables are filled with various baskets and some framed sports memorabilia, courtesy of the Stampede.

Scarlett stops in front of an item that contains two tickets to a wine tasting and a basket of bath salts. "That's not a prize; that's a cry for help."

I chuckle.

We stroll along, stopping at a basket labeled *A Night of Romance*. There's a candle shaped like a rose, a bottle of wine, and a leather-bound copy of *Pride and Prejudice*.

I glance at her, already smirking. "Tell me this isn't your idea of hell."

She arches a brow. "A scented candle, lukewarm cabernet, and a man with commitment issues? It's practically my autobiography."

I laugh, full and genuine. "You should write taglines for a living."

"I do write for a living."

"Right. Books about how I'm the enemy."

"Not you specifically," she says, then pauses. "But also not *not* you."

I pretend to clutch my heart. "Wounded."

"You'll live." She steps closer to the table, skimming a finger over the wine label. "Though, for the record, I'm more of a whiskey girl."

"Of course you are." I lean in just enough for her to notice. "Whiskey, biting sarcasm, and a total disregard for small talk. You're my dream woman."

She blinks once. Then twice.

A small smile pulls at her lips.

And maybe it's the champagne, maybe it's the suit, maybe it's the way she looks tonight—flawless, untouchable, and yet somehow the most *real* thing in this whole room—but I swear, for half a second, she actually looks like she's enjoying herself.

She turns to walk away, and I follow, still grinning like an idiot.

We stop in front of another auction item—this one a framed jersey signed by half the team. She eyes it with mild disinterest, as if she's trying to pretend she doesn't notice my name stitched across the back.

"You bidding?" I ask, nudging her lightly with my elbow.

She crosses her arms. "Please. I already have one just like it."

I blink. "You do?"

She nods, expression smug. "I use it to clean my windows. Works great on streaks."

I choke on a laugh. "Ouch. Ruthless."

Seriously, women don't speak to me like this. She's unreal—*mean*, even. So why do I like it so much?

She shrugs, clearly pleased with herself. "Just trying to keep your ego at bay."

I chuckle, then glance over at her. Her champagne's almost gone, her shoulders are a little more relaxed, and for a split second, she's not glaring at me.

Which feels like my cue.

I tilt my head, voice lower now. "So, when are you going to let me take you out on a proper date?"

Her reaction is immediate—a laugh, dry and sharp, followed by an eye roll that could knock over a grown man.

"Nice try," she says, setting her glass down on a nearby table. "But I don't do *proper dates*. Or *improper ones*, for that matter."

"Come on," I say, playing it easy, letting my smile linger. "Just one night. No obligations. I'll even behave."

She gives me a look. "You? Behave? That's not a date—that's science fiction."

"You're dodging the question."

"I'm rejecting the premise."

I shake my head, amused. "Alright. I'll try again later."

"You won't get a different answer."

"Still worth a shot."

She walks off, and I let her go—this time.

Because yeah, she brushed me off.

But the smile tugging at the corner of her

mouth?

That said maybe.

And *maybe* is more than enough for me.

I'm stretched out in bed, one foot under Rip's massive body as he snores at the far end like he personally pays the mortgage on this place. My tux jacket is slung over a chair, and my bow tie sits on the dresser.

The gala was a blur—good food, too many cameras, and one woman in an emerald dress who nearly stopped my heart.

I should be asleep, but I'm still too keyed up. It's not every day I beg for a date only to be turned down cold.

I can't help but wonder if Scarlett's lying awake thinking about me too. I decide to text her—under the guise of being friendly.

> Me: *You make it home okay?*

When my phone buzzes, I nearly fling it off the bed trying to grab it.

> Scarlett: *Sure did. I nearly pulled a muscle trying to get my Spanx off, but I'm all tucked into bed now.*

> Me: *Spanx?*

I scratch my chin. Am I supposed to know what that is?

Scarlett: *It's shapewear. You know what... never mind.*

Me: *Whatever it is, I'm sure you don't need it.*

She doesn't reply, and I'm not sure if I've said too much. Or maybe she's just tired. Then, a few minutes later... a new text.

Scarlett: *Don't let this go to your head, but... I think I might be ready for that date.*

I blink, reread it. Once. Twice. Then sit up because the weight of Rip's heavy body is suddenly not enough to keep me grounded.

Me: *Are you saying you want to go out with me?*

There's a pause, and I swear time slows.

Scarlett: *Don't ruin it, Remington.*

I grin like an idiot.

No way I'm letting this moment happen over text.

I hit call.

She picks up on the third ring. "If this is you gloating—"

"You're damn right it is."

She laughs, the sound warm and a little breathless. "I knew I shouldn't have said anything."

"You absolutely should have. I want it on record. Official documentation."

"I've been thinking…" she says, quieter now. "That maybe I wouldn't hate going on that date you mentioned."

I lay back, smiling at the ceiling like a complete fool. "That's the most romantic thing anyone's ever said to me."

"Shut up and pick a place," she mutters, but there's no heat in it—just that soft undercurrent she tries so hard to hide. The one that tells me she might be just as curious about this as I am.

I nudge Rip's ear. "Hear that, bud? We're in."

Rip groans.

Scarlett snorts. "Is that your dog?"

"He's very invested in our love story."

"Well, tell him to get used to disappointment."

I laugh. "Don't threaten him. He's fragile."

She's quiet for a second. Then, "Goodnight, Chase."

"Goodnight, Scarlett."

I hang up and stare at the phone for a long minute, wondering what the hell just shifted between us.

Whatever it was—I like it.

And I'm not blowing it.

Not this time.

26

AXE ME OUT SOMETIME

Scarlett

When I agreed to go out with Chase, I was fully prepared to regret it.

Not because he's a bad guy—well, okay, he *is* a cocky, insufferably smug hockey player with too much charm and not enough humility—but because this? This is a terrible idea.

He's the exact kind of guy I write *against*. The kind who coasts on confidence and looks. The kind who doesn't believe in quiet evenings or emotional depth. The kind who ruins perfectly reasonable, independent women with his dimples and devil-may-care swagger.

So imagine my surprise when I show up, expecting some overpriced steakhouse with a wine list longer than my last book—and instead, I find myself standing in front of a warehouse-looking building with a neon sign that reads:

AXE ME ANYTHING.

"You're joking," I say as I climb out of the car, eyeing the building like it personally offended me.

Chase leans against his Jeep, arms crossed, looking far too pleased with himself. "What, not fancy enough for you?"

"I thought you were going to wine and dine me."

"I thought about it. But I figured that wouldn't impress you."

"Smart boy."

He grins. "Plus, I like my eyebrows. Didn't feel like getting them burned off by your death glare over duck confit."

It's an interesting choice.

My only clue was when I texted him to ask about the dress code for tonight; he'd told me to wear sensible shoes.

It was a strange request. Not one I'd ever had from a date before. Not that I'd dated much in the last decade. But still.

He ushers me inside, and it's... actually kind of cool? Exposed brick walls, strings of Edison lights, and about six lanes of people hurling axes into wooden targets like it's a totally normal Saturday night.

"I swear to you," I murmur as I pick up a waiver, "if this is some kind of elaborate plan to off me,

I hope you know I've texted my location to multiple people."

"Please," he says. "If I wanted to kill you, I'd at least have the decency to wait until *after* dessert."

"You're a real gentleman, Remington."

"So they say," he hums, signing his own waiver with a flourish.

We're given a rundown by a very peppy employee named Jasmine who has safety goggles and the enthusiasm of a camp counselor on Red Bull. She walks us through the basics, shows us the right stance, and then hands us each an axe.

"Ready?" Chase asks, twirling his like it's *not* a literal weapon.

Jeez.

My stomach does a weird little flip.

"Born ready." I adjust my grip and square my shoulders, trying to remember what Jasmine said about follow-through.

"Ladies first." He gestures for me to begin.

My first throw goes wildly left.

"Okay, that was a warm-up," I say, brushing my hair out of my face.

"Sure it was."

"Don't get cocky."

"I'm literally just standing here."

He steps up, winds back, and sticks it dead center.

Of course he does.

I scowl. "You practice this in your off time?"

"Nah. I'm just naturally talented." He winks.

I hate how attractive I find that wink. Seriously... *annoying!*

I throw again. It thuds into the board but falls off.

"Form's solid," he says, stepping behind me. "You just need more momentum."

"Don't you dare give me a lesson."

"Too late." He moves in closer, positioning himself just behind me, and I can't help but be aware of his tall, muscular frame brushing my backside. Holy distracting! He smells incredible, and he's so big and warm behind me. He casually adjusts my grip on the handle. "Here. Pull back like this."

His hands are warm on mine, his breath brushes the side of my neck, and suddenly the air feels ten degrees hotter.

"This is a bad idea," I mutter.

"Which part?"

"Letting you this close to an axe."

He chuckles, low and amused. "Relax. I'm not the enemy tonight."

"I don't trust you with that kind of power."

"Fine," he says, stepping back. "But if you hurl that thing through the wall, I'm not explaining it to Jasmine."

I try again—and this time, it hits. Not the bullseye, but it sticks.

I turn to Chase, triumphant. "See? I don't need your help."

"You sure about that?" His voice is soft, teasing—but something else lingers there too.

I try not to notice the way his eyes drop to my mouth. Try not to notice the way my heart thumps like a warning bell.

We play a few more rounds, the trash talk flying easily between us, and for a while, it's easy. Fun, even. No pressure. No book club. No audience.

Just us.

Eventually, we turn in our axes, and he grabs my hand like it's the most natural thing in the world, tugging me toward the door. "Come on."

I narrow my eyes. "Where are we going now?"

"You'll see."

"You already tried to kill me once tonight."

"Technically, you tried to kill yourself with your throwing technique."

He drives us five minutes out of town to a little hill overlooking the lake. The stars are out in full force, scattered across the sky like confetti, and there's a tiny food truck parked near the edge of the lot.

"Is this part two of your murder plot?"

"Nope." He parks, orders two milkshakes from the vendor, and hands me one. "Peanut butter for you. Strawberry for me."

I blink. "You remembered that?"

He shrugs. "I pay attention."

I don't know what to do with that.

So I take a sip.

And damn it—it's perfect. Seriously, if I ever get sent to death row, this exact milkshake would be my final meal request. It's life-changing.

Damn him.

We sit on the hood of the Jeep, the stars above us, treetops swishing in the distance, and it's… quiet. Peaceful.

Too peaceful.

Because the more silent it gets, the more I hear my own heartbeat, loud and traitorous.

Chase looks over at me. "So… not the date you expected?"

"No," I say softly. "It's better."

He smiles. Not smug. Not teasing.

Just… soft.

Real.

And in that moment, I'm not Scottie Calloway, self-proclaimed cynic and author of anti-love literature.

I'm just a girl sitting on a Jeep, next to a guy who sees me in a way I wasn't ready for.

And worse?

I think I kind of like it.

We finish our shakes slower than necessary, both of us drawing out the moment like we know something about it matters. I don't say that out loud, obviously, because that would require vulnerability and honesty and other horrifying things. But I feel it hanging in the air between us.

I'm not as immune as I like to pretend.

The night is warm, but not hot. Crickets hum in the distance. There's a slight breeze and plenty of stars.

And Chase smells like cedar and clean laundry and something vaguely citrusy. It's unfair how good he smells, especially when I'm trying very hard not to be charmed.

"So," I say, because silence is dangerous. "You grew up in Michigan, you said?"

"Just outside Grand Rapids," he says, sipping the last of his strawberry milkshake. "Small town. Lots of ponds, one decent diner, and a high school hockey team that thought it was the NHL."

I smile into my straw. "Let me guess. You were the star."

"I peaked early," he says dryly. "Now I just get paid to smash into people and skate in circles."

I laugh, but he's watching me, expression a little softer now.

"What about you?" he asks. "Chicago girl, right?"

"Born and raised."

"You ever miss it?"

"Sometimes," I admit. "Mostly the food. And

the lakefront. And… maybe who I was before everything got complicated."

He leans back on his elbows, his long legs stretched in front of him. "That happen young? The complications?"

I glance up at the stars. "Yeah. Unfortunately, my childhood memories are tinged with lots of fighting. Before the divorce. Before my dad left and my mom stopped trying."

He's quiet, listening in a way most people don't.

"That's probably why I'm so… cynical," I add. "It's hard to believe in love when the people who were supposed to model it for you couldn't get it right."

He doesn't rush to fill the space. When he finally speaks, his voice is quiet. "Between that and the end of your relationship… it left a mark."

"It left a mark," I repeat softly.

We sit in silence for a beat.

Then he says, "I think that's why I don't usually date. Or… attach, I guess. It's easier to stay focused when you don't let anyone close."

I raise a brow. "Funny. That's my entire brand."

He glances over at me. "So what are we doing here, then?"

I look at him. The lights from the food truck are behind us now, and his face is lit only by the moon and stars. His hair's a little messy. His expression is unreadable.

"I don't know," I whisper.

And then he kisses me.

It's soft at first—hesitant, like he's giving me a chance to pull away.

I don't.

His hand finds my jaw, his fingers brush lightly behind my ear, and I lean in instinctively, letting myself feel it. The press of his lips. The warmth of his palm. The way the world fades out, just for a second, until there's nothing left but this.

Him.

Us.

He deepens the kiss and oh wow, I feel a zing of pleasure course through me.

That's new.

He tastes like strawberry ice cream, and his tongue is very, *very* persuasive. I forget all the reasons why I was opposed to him in the first place. In fact, I forget everything…my name, my zip code, the entire concept of self-control.

When he pulls back, I blink, dazed.

And then he clears his throat and shifts back in his seat.

"Okay," he says, his voice slightly unsteady. "I better, uh, take you home."

I stare at him.

"What?" I ask, still breathless. "That's it?"

He laughs under his breath. "Trust me. If I stay

here another minute, I'm going to make that kiss a whole lot more complicated."

My heart pounds in a way that's both exhilarating and terrifying.

He stands and offers his hand to help me off the Jeep hood.

I take it.

And I don't say anything else the whole ride home—because honestly? I'm not sure what just happened either.

But something did.

And I'm not sure I'll ever be the same.

Harper once bet me I wouldn't last the summer without falling for Chase Remington. I laughed in her face. And yet… here I am. Lipstick smudged. Heart racing. Sad that our date is over.

What's happening to me?

27
Plot Twists & Pastries
Scarlett

The sun is too bright, the coffee smells too good, and I'm smiling. Like... actually smiling.

Which is *suspicious*.

Harper narrows her eyes the second I slide into the booth across from her at the little indie café we always meet at. She's already got two croissants on a plate and a cappuccino halfway gone.

"You're ten minutes late," she says.

I shrug, tugging off my sunglasses. "I walked."

"In heeled boots?"

"They're barely heeled. Also, why are you squinting at me like I just confessed to murder?"

Her eyes narrow further. "You're in a *mood*."

I sip my coffee innocently. "Maybe I'm just enjoying the day."

"No, see, this is *suspiciously chipper* for someone who was in a full spiral just a few days ago. You *hated* everyone and everything. You told me love was a scam and you wanted to disappear into the woods and live off-grid."

"I still stand by that. Mostly." I push my hair over one shoulder.

She leans in, grinning. "Something happened. You're glowing. Like, annoyingly so. I need to know everything immediately."

I open my mouth to lie—because I *was* going to lie—but the words slip out faster than I can stop them.

"I went on a date."

"WHAT?!" she roars.

I turn an unflattering shade of red as the people around us glance over. "Lower your voice," I hiss.

Her jaw drops. "With *Chase*?"

I pretend to study the foam art in my latte. "It wasn't a big deal."

Harper smacks the table. "*Scarlett Louise Calloway.*"

I wince. "I know, okay? I don't know what happened. One minute we were fighting over his taste in books, the next we were throwing axes and drinking milkshakes under the stars."

Her jaw is *still* on the floor.

"And?"

"And it was… good," I admit. "*Really* good."

Harper exhales dramatically. "Okay, forget the

book. We need to talk about this man."

I roll my eyes, but I can't help the smile tugging at my lips. "There's nothing to talk about. It was *one* date. That's it. Probably won't be a repeat; we're definitely *not* walking down the aisle. I'm not giving up my independence, goals, and dreams for a guy who slaps around a rubber puck for a living."

She doesn't look convinced.

She's looking at me like this is a Disney movie.

"Breathe, Harper," I remind her, taking another sip of my latte.

"Uh huh. Just one date and suddenly you're skipping through Dallas like a Disney princess on espresso."

"I'm not *skipping*."

"You're emotionally skipping."

I laugh, then pause—because her words settle somewhere in my chest.

It *was* different last night. I felt... lighter. And maybe a little *seen*, which is terrifying in its own right. But who knows, maybe this is what growth looks like? Just getting out of your own head long enough to do something different.

Harper takes another bite of her croissant and eyes me carefully. "So... are you gonna see him again?"

"I don't know," I say honestly. "He kind of ended things abruptly."

Her brows shoot up. "What do you mean?"

"I mean, we kissed. But after? He pulled back. Said he better take me home. Like *he* was the one drawing boundaries."

Harper stares at me, stunned. "Well damn. I think I like him now."

I groan. "Don't say that."

"You already do," she says, with a knowing look.

I flip her off, and she laughs, victorious.

After a beat, she says, "So what about the book?"

I sober instantly. "I… actually have an idea."

She stills. "Wait, really?"

I nod, picking at the corner of my napkin. "It's nothing like anything I've written before. It's scary and soft and hopeful and maybe… a little bit romantic?"

Her eyes widen.

"I don't even know where it came from," I mumble. "It just hit me after the other night. But it's so off-brand, it might tank everything I've built."

She doesn't hesitate. "Or it could be the best thing you've ever written."

I glance up.

"I mean it," she says gently. "You're not the same person you were when you started writing those books. Maybe this is your next chapter."

The lump in my throat is unexpected.

"I don't know if I'm brave enough to write it," I admit.

She reaches across the table and squeezes my hand. "You are."

And for the first time in a long time… I *almost* believe her.

The air's crisp as I step out of the coffee shop, latte in hand, still thinking about Harper's relentless optimism. The girl could put a positive spin on an IRS audit. I love her for it. I hate her for it.

Mostly, I wish I believed her.

The bookstore across the street catches my eye, but I keep walking, not ready to risk seeing a display of hockey-themed romance novels with my face awkwardly Photoshopped next to Chase's. Instead, I duck into a boutique I don't recognize— one of those beachy, boho places with soft lighting and too many mirrors.

A little bell chimes overhead as I enter, and the scent of jasmine and expensive leather hits me immediately. Everything in here is stupidly pretty. Delicate. Soft.

Not usually my thing, but I'm already here, so I decide to look around.

Dresses. Tops. Flowy skirts I'd never wear unless I was running barefoot through a vineyard. I tell myself I'm just killing time, that it's research for future character building or some other lie.

And then I see it.

A slip dress.

Midnight blue. Satin. Bias-cut and delicate without being frilly. The kind of dress that doesn't try too hard. The kind of dress that says: I didn't come to impress you, but go ahead and be impressed.

I reach out before I can stop myself. Let my fingers trail the fabric. It's... lovely.

"Want to try it on?" the salesgirl asks, appearing beside me.

I almost say no.

But then—I don't.

Inside the dressing room, I slide the dress over my head, and for a minute, I just stare.

Not because I look incredible.

Not because I'm suddenly transformed.

But because I don't hate what I see.

There's something about the way the fabric clings to me—unapologetically. It reminds me of something I haven't felt in a while.

Desire.

Not for anyone else.

For myself.

I stand a little straighter. Smooth the fabric over my hips. And I know—I'm buying this damn dress.

Not for Chase.

Not for a photoshoot or an event or the fans.

For me.

Maybe I am a little different lately.

And maybe that doesn't have to be such a bad thing.

Harper once bet me that I'd fall for Chase. At the time, I brushed it off as ridiculous. Now, I'm starting to see how easily a girl could fall for him... And that scares me.

Letting my walls down won't be easy. But it might be worth it.

Back at my condo, the afternoon light spills across the living room in soft golden stripes. I toss my keys into the bowl by the door, drop the shopping bag on the couch, and then... hover.

I grab the bag.

A few minutes later, I'm standing in front of my full-length mirror, barefoot on the hardwood floor, slipping the dress back over my head. It falls into place like it belongs there. Like *I* belong in it.

It's soft. And sleek. And scandalous in a way that feels quietly powerful.

I smooth my hands over the fabric. Tilt my head.

And—okay—maybe I *do* look a little amazing.

I grab my phone, still uncertain why. Snap a photo. Nothing too extra. Just enough to say: *Is this a terrible decision or my best one yet?*

I almost send it to Harper.

Almost.

Instead... my thumb hovers.

And then I scroll to another name.

Chase.
I don't overthink it.
I just type.

Scarlett: *Should I return this?*

I attach the photo.
Thumb hovers over the send button.
I send it anyway.
Immediately regret it.
Pace the room once. Twice.
Then—

Chase: *Holy hell.*

Do not return that.

Ever.

I laugh, one hand pressed to my mouth, heart thudding like an idiot.
And for the first time in a long time…
I don't feel ridiculous for wanting to be seen.
Just maybe?
I want to be seen *by him.*

28

SEND HELP. I CAUGHT FEELINGS

Chase

We land in Arizona around midnight, and I'm still grinning like an idiot.

Not because we just stomped the Kings on their home ice—though, yeah, we did. And not because I scored two goals and assisted on a third—though that was pretty great too.

No, I'm grinning because I can't stop thinking about Scarlett.

Specifically, the way she looked trash-talking me at axe throwing—despite the fact that she was losing—badly.

The way she looked when she tasted the peanut butter milkshake—eyes drifting closed—like it was pure happiness. And I put that look there. Me.

The way her voice had gone quiet—just for a second—when she talked about her parents. About the lake house. About the before and after.

And that kiss?

That kiss wrecked me.

Soft, then not-so-soft. Curious, then sure. It was a kiss that didn't just *mean* something—it *changed* something.

Basically, I'm screwed.

"You're smiling again," Tyler says from the hotel bed across from mine. He's scrolling through TikTok like it's a competitive sport. "You got a secret girlfriend, or are you just pleased with yourself?"

"Both," I mutter.

He looks over, eyes narrowing. "Oh damn, am I about to lose that bet?"

I'd almost forgotten about that stupid wager we'd made. Tyler didn't think I could get the Ice Queen to agree to a date, and yeah, I guess I did. "I'm not collecting on that bet, dude. That was a *joke*."

"Okay, so you and Scottie Calloway. Huh." He scratches his facial hair. "I didn't think you had it in you."

I'm not one to kiss and tell, especially not with something as fragile as me and Scarlett. I don't know if she'll even agree to a second date.

Though something tells me she will.

"You guys hook up?"

I hurl a pillow at him.

He ducks, laughing. "You're scoring more than usual, and this time, I actually mean on the ice."

"Shut up."

"You shut up. You've been skating like you've got rockets in your skates. Whatever she's doing to your game, keep letting her do it."

I roll onto my back, stare at the ceiling.

He's not wrong. Something's clicked. I'm lighter on my feet. Sharper. More focused.

Because for the first time in a while, I'm not chasing the next distraction. I'm thinking about *her.*

I'm thinking about the way her pulse fluttered in her neck when I leaned in to kiss her. The way her fingers curled into the front of my shirt like she didn't want to let go.

And yeah, I didn't want to let go either.

Which is a problem.

Because she's not just any girl. She's Scottie freaking Calloway—the woman who built a career on calling love a scam.

And I'm the one she kissed.

So now I'm lying here in this stupid hotel bed, supposed to be resting before our next game, and instead, I'm thinking about her lips, her laugh, and that look in her eyes when she let her walls down just enough for me to see inside.

I fish my phone off the nightstand.

Scroll to our text thread.

She hasn't messaged since she sent me that photo of her in a dress.

I haven't either.

We're in that weird space between—what are we, exactly?

Still enemies? Definitely not.

Friends? Maybe.

More?

I want to find out.

But not through a screen.

So I tuck the phone away, close my eyes, and let my mind drift back to that kiss.

Yeah.

I am *so* screwed.

29

THINGS THAT CATCH FIRE

Chase

Scarlett is sitting on my kitchen counter, legs swinging, hair twisted up in some messy knot that's making it really hard to focus on the task at hand.

Which is—not setting the kitchen on fire.

"I thought you said you knew how to cook," she says, eyeing the smoke curling up from the pan like she's already planning her escape route.

"I do," I say confidently, even as the smoke alarm starts to beep. "Mostly."

Rip is lying in the corner, head on his paws, watching this whole disaster unfold like he's seen it a hundred times. Which he has.

Scarlett hops down from the counter, waving a dish towel at the smoke alarm while laughing. "Should I call for backup? Or maybe a pizza?"

"You're seriously underestimating my capabilities," I mutter, grabbing the skillet and trying to salvage what used to be chicken.

"You're seriously *overestimating* your stove settings."

I roll my eyes.

Eventually, I manage to get dinner on the table—somewhat charred chicken tacos, homemade guac that turned out suspiciously decent, and store-bought churros I tried to pass off as handmade until she caught the price tag still on the box.

We eat on the couch, Rip wedged between us like the world's fluffiest chaperone, while a low-fi playlist hums in the background. Scarlett's curled up with her knees tucked under her, a taco in one hand and a margarita in the other.

"This is fun," she says, and I glance over, surprised by how soft her voice sounds.

"Even with the almost-fire?"

She grins. "Especially with the almost-fire."

I'm just glad she agreed to come over.

She takes a sip of her drink, then nudges my knee with hers. "So. How was the road trip?"

"Exhausting," I say. "California, Arizona, back-to-back games. But good. We won both."

"Look at you. A functioning adult with a winning streak."

"Shocking, I know."

She gives me a look.

I shrug, trying to downplay it. "Yeah, I felt good on the ice. Fast. Focused."

She studies me for a second. "You've been playing really well lately. I read that stat thing online. Your coach said something about how you've stepped into a leadership role."

I glance away, caught off guard by the pride in her voice. "Yeah, well. Trying not to screw it up."

"You won't," she says simply, like it's a fact.

I glance over. "You sure about that?"

"Pretty sure." She pops the last bite of her taco into her mouth.

Next, she asks about my parents, and I ask about the first book she ever wrote. She tells me about her writing process—equal parts caffeine, panic, and Google Docs. I tell her about the time I accidentally texted my coach instead of my dog-sitter and invited him to stay in my guest room.

It's easy.

We navigate between deeper topics and amusing ones like it's nothing.

By the time we're done eating, the sky outside has darkened. She's sitting beside me now, close enough that her bare leg brushes mine every time she shifts. My hand is draped along the back of the couch, fingers itching to reach for her.

She catches me staring, and her lips curve. "What?"

"Nothing." I shrug. "You just…fit here. Better

than I thought you would."

Her smile falters for half a second, then softens. "I'm not staying the night, if that's what you're thinking."

I laugh. "Didn't say you were. Although Rip would be thrilled."

At the sound of his name, Rip lifts his head and promptly rests it in Scarlett's lap with a dramatic sigh.

"Betrayal," I mutter.

Scarlett scratches behind his ears. "You'll live."

I lean forward, nudging her foot with mine. "Want another churro?"

She hesitates for a second, then nods.

I go grab them, and when I come back, she's tucked under a blanket, Rip still using her as a pillow, and she looks so ridiculously at home that something shifts in my chest. A little jolt, like maybe I'm not just falling for her—I already have.

I hand her the churro.

She arches a brow. "Is this how you woo women? Flammable dinners and pre-packaged desserts?"

"It's a high-risk, high-reward strategy."

She takes a bite. "Well. You're lucky I have low standards."

I smirk. "Noted."

We fall into a comfortable conversation, with the sound of Rip snoring and the soft hum of music.

And for the first time in a long time, my house doesn't feel like just a place I sleep.

It feels like something more.

It feels like her.

I don't know how long I've been staring at her. Probably too long. Definitely too long.

Her lips are parted, her cheeks a little flushed. There's something soft in her eyes now—unguarded.

I shift slightly, resting my arm on the back of the couch behind her.

"You tired?" I ask.

She shakes her head, her voice barely above a whisper. "Not yet."

I nod slowly. "Cool."

Because I am smooth. And articulate. And absolutely not spiraling internally over whether this is a moment or not.

Scarlett turns to me, curling her legs a little closer to her body, one hand brushing back a loose strand of hair. "Why are you looking at me like that?"

I blink. "Like what?"

"Like I'm going to disappear."

I don't answer. I can't. Because that's exactly what it feels like. Like if I don't hold on tight enough, she'll vanish.

She swallows. "Say something."

So I do.

"You drive me insane," I murmur. "And I can't stop wanting you, even when I know I might end up hurt."

Her breath catches.

I lean in—slowly, giving her time to pull away if she wants. But she doesn't. Her eyes flicker to my mouth, then back to my eyes.

She whispers, "You're not supposed to make me feel like this."

My voice is low. "Like what?"

"Like maybe I've been wrong about everything."

That's all the permission I need.

I close the space between us, pressing my lips to hers—slow, tentative, like I'm afraid to want it too much.

But then she kisses me back.

And it's not slow anymore.

It's soft, then demanding. Her fingers curl in my shirt, and my hand slides up to cradle her jaw, angling her closer like I need her in every way a person can need someone.

The blanket slips to the floor. Rip snorts in protest and jumps down, giving us a wide berth as Scarlett shifts to straddle my lap, her hands threading through my hair.

She tastes like cinnamon and sugar and something I've been craving for a very long time.

She kisses like she argues—fierce, unwavering, and absolutely certain she's going to win.

When we finally pull apart, her breath is shaky. Mine's wrecked, too.

Her forehead rests against mine.

"Well," she murmurs, her voice low and still a little breathless, "that was… really good."

I grin, still catching my breath. "Yeah?"

She nods, but her lips twitch into a smirk. "Bonus points for actually knowing how to kiss. I wasn't convinced you would."

I laugh, leaning in to press my lips against hers again. "You were testing me?"

She shrugs, eyes dancing. "Consider it a trial run. I guess you'll do."

"You *guess* I'll do?" I echo, mock-offended. That's a first.

She arches a brow, smug. "Don't get cocky."

"Too late," I murmur, kissing her again.

And this time, she doesn't pull away.

And she might not be ready to say it out loud— but that? That was her letting me in.

And I'm not going anywhere.

30

THIS IS NOT A DATE (BUT I SHAVED MY LEGS ANYWAY)

Scarlett

I stare into my full-length mirror like it just personally offended me.

The maxi dress that Amazon promised looks good on everyone looks like a sack on me.

Ultra flattering, my ass. Seriously, I look like I'm wearing a diaper underneath it.

I toss it straight into the pile of other Amazon returns that must go back this week and grab a pair of jeans and a cream-colored sweater.

Because I shouldn't be overthinking this.

I'm going to a coffee shop. To work. With a guy who makes my heart race and my brain melt and who kissed me like it meant something—which, for the record, is *not* something I should still be thinking about days later.

But I am.

Unfortunately.

I tug on the soft, oversized sweater and glance in the mirror, then promptly yank it off again. Too cozy. Too much like *I'm trying to look cute without trying to look cute.*

Which, okay—maybe I am. But still.

Next comes a sleek black top that hugs my waist a little too nicely. I scowl. Off.

I finally land on a gray V-neck and my favorite jeans. Safe. Neutral. Not date-worthy.

Because this isn't a date.

We're just… working together. I told him I needed to write a little bit today, and he promised he'd let me work while he got some of his own stuff done.

So, see? Not a date.

I add a swipe of mascara anyway. Just… for my lashes.

My phone buzzes.

Chase: *On my way. Try not to miss me too much.*

I snort. Out loud.

My heart does a dumb little flip anyway.

I grab my laptop, shove it into my tote bag, and march out the door before I can think myself into another spiral.

Besides, I've got words to write, coffee to drink, and exactly zero time to wonder what it means that I can't stop smiling every time he texts me.

Not a date.

Totally fine.

Everything's fine.

The little bell above the coffee shop door jingles as I step inside, the familiar scent of espresso and warm baked goods wrapping around me like a hug I didn't ask for but kind of needed.

It's bustling but not packed—just enough background chatter to feel lively, not overwhelming.

I spot him instantly.

Chase is at a corner table, already sipping a coffee, laptop open, brows drawn in concentration. His hair's still damp from a shower, curling slightly at the ends, and he's wearing a dark hoodie pushed up at the sleeves, exposing his forearms in a way that should absolutely not be legal before noon.

He hasn't seen me yet.

Which means I have a solid ten seconds to get my heartbeat under control.

Because he looks good.

Too good.

And I'm annoyed about it.

I head toward the counter, order my usual, and by the time I make my way to the table, he looks up—and grins like I just made his whole morning.

"Hey," he says, voice warm. "You made it."

"Obviously," I reply, sliding into the seat across from him. "I was promised caffeine and chaos."

He chuckles, pushing a scone toward me. "I got your favorite. Figured it would soften your contempt."

I eye it suspiciously. "You bribing me, Remington?"

"Always."

We settle in. I open my laptop, determined to focus, but there's a strange sort of... energy buzzing between us. Comfortable. Charged. Like we've slipped into something familiar without realizing it.

"So," I say, pretending not to care, "what are you working on?"

"Team stuff," he replies, running a hand through his hair. "They've got me prepping this leadership pitch for captain. Presentation, goals, ideas on team culture. I swear, I didn't know hockey came with PowerPoint."

I blink. "You're making a PowerPoint? That's... shockingly responsible of you."

"I know," he says, mock solemn. "Please hold your applause."

I smirk, taking another sip. "Well, I'm proud of you, Remington. Look at you. All grown up and goal-oriented."

He leans back, eyes on me. "You bring out my best."

It's so smooth, I almost choke on my sip of coffee.

"I'm going to pretend I didn't hear that," I mutter.

"You loved it."

My cheeks flush.

I busy myself with typing, and after a beat, the only sounds are the soft clacks of our keyboards and the occasional hum of espresso machines. This new book idea is actually flowing.

But he's still looking at me. I can feel it.

"What?" I ask without glancing up.

"You look happy," he says, quiet now.

I freeze.

"Like, writing-happy. It's a good look on you." And just like that, my walls threaten to crumble. Because no one's ever noticed that before.

I lift my gaze to meet his.

"Thanks," I murmur.

And somehow, without meaning to, this not-a-date feels like so much more.

The coffee shop is warm and bustling, full of soft indie music, clinking mugs, and the faint scent of espresso.

And the guy sitting across from me is an annoyingly attractive temptation. Baseball cap backward, hoodie pushed to his elbows, a pen in his mouth as he studies something on his tablet like it holds the meaning of life.

Focus, Scottie.

I get to work, and soon, I'm in the zone.

"Are you going to let me read what you're writing?" he asks a little while later.

I consider it for half a second before shaking my head. "I never let anyone read a work in progress. Sorry."

He leans back. "That's fine. It's just... you've got this glow about you. I can tell you like what you're writing."

I feel my cheeks warm and promptly focus on my keyboard. "I do not have a glow."

"You do," he says, very sure of himself. "It's cute."

I glance up at him. "You're cute."

His brows shoot up.

"...I mean in a golden retriever way," I add quickly.

"Uh-huh," he says, clearly enjoying this.

We go back to working, the air between us charged in that quiet, content way. My fingers fly across the keyboard, the words coming like a faucet finally turned back on. I know exactly what this character is feeling. I know how she's falling even though she doesn't want to.

I'll be honest, I had my doubts if I could get much done with him today, but I've already written 1,000 words. Not bad.

Across the table, Chase's pen is moving again,

scribbling notes. He catches me looking.

"What?" he says with a smirk.

"Nothing," I say too quickly.

He raises a brow. "You checking me out, Calloway?"

"Nope." I busy myself with my scone—breaking off a hunk and shoving it in my mouth.

"Thanks," I say quietly.

"For the scone?" he teases.

"For this," I say, gesturing between us.

An hour later, we both start packing up at the same time, him stretching with a groan as he shuts his laptop.

"Productive morning," he says, grabbing our empty mugs to return to the counter. "I only made three memes in the team group chat and rewrote the same paragraph six times."

I smirk as I slip my laptop into my tote. "I wrote an entire chapter and only freaked out once. So, really, we're both thriving."

"Look at us," he says, holding the door open for me as we step into the warm Dallas afternoon. "Functioning adults with goals and everything. It's disgusting."

I laugh, and it feels easy. Too easy. Which should probably concern me.

He falls into step beside me as we stroll toward the parking lot, his hand brushing mine for a second—just enough to make me hyperaware of how close we're walking.

"So," he says casually, "you remember that thing I invited you to?"

I blink. "You're gonna have to be more specific. You say a lot of things."

"The team dinner," he replies, nudging me with his elbow. "Tomorrow night. A few guys, some plus-ones, nothing too fancy. You in?"

I hesitate. It's one thing to spend time with *him*. It's another to waltz into a dinner with his teammates like… we're a thing.

He notices my pause and adds, "No pressure. I just figured you could use another excuse to judge my life choices in real time."

I raise a brow. "And what, exactly, would I be judging?"

"I don't know. The company I keep. The way I inhale wings like a feral animal. My ability to be both devastatingly handsome and marginally charming at the same time."

"You forgot humble."

"Obviously. That's my most consistent flaw."

I laugh despite myself. "I'll think about it."

He grins. "You'll come."

I shake my head. "You're insufferable."

"And yet, here you are."

I roll my eyes, unlocking my car.

"Text me when you get home," he says, backing toward his Jeep. "Just so I know you didn't get kidnapped."

I give him a mock salute. "Noted."

And as I slide into the driver's seat, I realize—
my cheeks hurt.

From smiling.

Damn it.

λ

31

COULD'VE FOOLED ME

Chase

It's already loud when we walk into the restaurant—one of those places with exposed brick walls, moody lighting, and way too many flat screens playing highlight reels none of us are actually watching. We've got a big corner table, and most of the team is already there, shouting over each other and giving our poor waitress the runaround.

Scarlett pauses just inside the door, scanning the chaos like she's evaluating whether or not this was a colossal mistake. I nudge her with my elbow.

"You can still run," I murmur. "Fake an emergency. Say you left your straightener on."

She tilts her head at me. "You'd just chase me down."

"You say that like it's a bad thing."

She rolls her eyes, but I catch the way her lips twitch, like she's trying not to smile.

As we walk toward the table, Rip's name is the first thing I hear—Tyler is midway through a dramatic reenactment of the time Rip stole a hot dog straight out of his hand during a team barbecue.

"He didn't even hesitate," Tyler says, eyes wide. "Just walked up like he owned my ass and *took it*. I'm still not over it."

Scarlett laughs, and suddenly I'm not the only one watching her. Heads turn. Smirks form.

Bennett lifts a brow as we approach. "Well, well. If it isn't the *actual* queen of heartbreak."

I groan. "We said we weren't calling her that anymore."

"She literally writes books telling women to leave us," Tyler says. "And somehow you're the one she shows up with?"

Scarlett shrugs as she takes the open seat next to me. "Chase is good for research."

The whole table howls. Even I have to give her that one.

"Scarlett, this is everyone," I say, motioning around the table. "Everyone, this is—"

"We know," Will cuts in. "We've seen the clips."

"And read the social media comments," adds Nolan.

"And watched the fan cam on YouTube," Bennett says with a completely straight face.

Scarlett sips her water like she's unfazed. "Glad to know I'm making an impression."

"You've got the team's stamp of approval," Bennett says, tossing me a look. "She's good for you, man."

Scarlett blinks. I feel her shift slightly beside me.

It wasn't said loudly. Wasn't some grand pronouncement.

Just a simple comment, tossed into the noise of team banter and bottomless fries.

But she heard it.

I did too.

The conversation moves on—back to hockey, and someone's fantasy football disaster, and who clogged the hotel bathroom on our last road trip (Tyler, obviously). But my attention keeps drifting back to her.

She's relaxed, laughing easily, holding her own like she's been doing this forever. No pretense. No snarky armor.

Just her.

I don't know when it happened. When *this* stopped being a PR stunt or a challenge or a bet and started feeling like the most natural thing in the world.

But watching her now—shoulder brushing mine, eyes lit with laughter—I know one thing for sure.

She belongs here.

And I'm not just talking about tonight.

We linger longer than we meant to—Scarlett and Lucy are deep in a conversation about a viral video from book club, and somehow Will's now trying to convince me Rip could be a professional dog model.

By the time we finally say our goodbyes and step outside, the air's cooled down just enough to be pleasant. The restaurant's twinkly patio lights stretch above us, and the soft hum of traffic fills the quiet.

I open the passenger door of my Jeep for her, but she doesn't climb in yet.

Instead, she leans against the frame, looking at me with that unreadable expression she wears way too well.

"What?" I ask.

Scarlett shrugs. "Just… I didn't hate that."

I smirk. "You sound surprised."

"I am." She crosses her arms. "I expected to be overwhelmed by testosterone and locker room jokes."

"Oh, there were definitely locker room jokes. You just missed 'em while Lucy was asking about your latest literary masterpiece."

Scarlett rolls her eyes, but she's smiling now.

We stand there for a second longer, neither of

us in a rush. Her arms are still crossed, her hair a little messy from the wind, and her eyes softer than usual.

"You're good at this," she says quietly.

I blink. "Good at what?"

"This. The team. The whole… people thing. You'll make a good captain. They look up to you. They listen when you talk."

My brows lift. "You thought I was just a dumb jock."

"I still think that," she deadpans.

But her tone is light, and I see it—the shift. The careful unraveling of her guard.

"I like seeing you like this," she adds, a little more seriously. "Not flirting. Not performing. Just… you."

It hits me right in the chest. The way she says it. The way she sees me.

Not for who I pretend to be.

But for who I am.

I step closer, sliding my hands into my pockets to keep from touching her. "I think that's the nicest thing you've ever said to me."

She smirks. "Don't get used to it."

"I won't," I say, but my voice is rougher now. Lower. "But for the record… you fit in with them."

Scarlett shakes her head. "I'm not a hockey girlfriend."

"Didn't say you were."

She looks up at me, something unreadable flickering behind her eyes.

"I just meant," I say, softer this time, "you belong. Wherever you want to be."

Her breath catches slightly, and for a split second, I wonder if I went too far.

But then she says, "You better take me home before I do something crazy."

My brows lift. "Define crazy."

"Like kiss you again."

My brain short-circuits.

"I mean, it wasn't terrible," she says with a shrug, stepping around me to climb into the passenger seat. "For a first date."

I laugh, full and low, and close her door behind her.

As I walk around to the driver's side, I swear—I've never wanted someone more.

32

CHAOS INCOMING

Scarlett

I fire off a text the second the plane touches down.

Me: *Just landed. I'll see you soon.*

My heart taps out a rhythm I'm pretending not to notice. It's not nerves. It's just… travel jitters. Normal adrenaline. Totally not because I'm about to spend the next three days sharing a hotel room with Chase Remington.

Chase: *Can't wait. Car should be waiting for you outside of baggage claim. Unless you chicken out…*

I smirk at my screen. Of course he's being a smartass. It helps. Keeps things from getting too serious, too fast.

Still, as I gather my things and shuffle off the plane, I'm hyperaware of everything. Of how this trip isn't just a "visit" or a "work thing."

It's a step.

A choice.

I could've said no. But I didn't.

I said yes.

Yes to the weekend. And yes to him.

I wait by baggage claim, trying not to fidget, running through a mental checklist. Outfits. Makeup. Laptop in case inspiration strikes. And—yep. Cute underwear. Just in case.

Not because I'm planning anything.

Just because… anything could happen.

I take a deep breath and shake the thought off. No sense in overthinking it. Otherwise, I'll completely panic. And we can't have that—not while I'm inside the airport, at least.

We have a team dinner tonight, which should be fun. I've gotten to know a couple of the guys, and he has a hockey game tomorrow. But the rest of the weekend? It'll be just us.

Outside, the air is colder than I expected—sharp and brisk with a city pulse that vibrates in my chest. A driver holding a sign that says "Calloway" waits in front of a black SUV.

Oh, we're doing full red carpet treatment now?

I slide into the backseat and sink into the plush leather, nerves fluttering wildly.

It's just a trip. Just a weekend. Just a hotel room.

But no matter how many times I repeat it... I know better.

This isn't *just* anything.

It's everything.

And I really, really hope I'm not making a mistake.

I spot Chase the second I step into the restaurant where we're meeting—tall and lean in a dark button-down, sleeves rolled to his elbows, hair pushed back like he ran his hands through it a dozen times waiting for me. He's standing just outside the private dining room, hands in his pockets, rocking slightly on his heels. Like he's nervous.

His whole face lights up when he sees me.

"Hi."

I don't get a chance to say hi back before he's pulling me in, arms wrapping around my waist. I press in without thinking, nose brushing his collarbone, and breathe him in—cologne and clean linen and something warm I can't quite name.

"You look—" His hand slips to my lower back as he leans back to really look at me. "Wow."

My cheeks flush instantly. "You're just saying that because I'm not in leggings and a sweatshirt for once."

"I'm saying it because it's true." His voice drops.

I laugh, and his mouth grazes my temple. It's

not quite a kiss, but close enough to make my chest tighten.

"How's it going in there?" I nod toward the dining room. "Any early fights break out over the appetizers?"

"Nah, it's shockingly civilized," he says, stepping back and sliding his hand into mine like it's the easiest thing in the world. "Come on, I'll get you a drink. Bar's right over here."

We walk past the open kitchen, the low thrum of conversation spilling out from the team and staff packed into the private room. Bennett catches my eye and grins. Lucy waves. The whole thing feels... almost normal. Like I belong here.

Is that crazy?

Maybe so, but I'm choosing to lean in.

Chase rests his hand on my lower back as we reach the bar. "What do you want? Wine? A cocktail? Whiskey?"

"Surprise me," I say, smiling.

He leans in like he's going to whisper a secret, but instead, he just brushes his lips against my cheek and says, "Dangerous words."

As he turns to flag down the bartender, I step back to wait, letting my eyes drift across the room. That's when I hear it.

"...thought he'd crack first," someone says, low and amused. "But turns out Remington's more stubborn than I gave him credit for."

"I mean, I didn't think she'd last this long either," comes the response, followed by a quiet laugh. "Honestly thought he'd fold after that bookstore stunt. She's got him whipped."

"Bet's still on, though. Week left. You in or out?"

My blood runs cold.

Tyler. Will.

I can't see them, but I know those voices. That easy, cocky tone. My stomach twists hard enough to hurt.

Bet.

The word rattles around in my head like a dropped marble.

A week left.

They're still talking about it. Still laughing about it. About *me*.

And Chase—Chase knew.

The blood drains from my face. I can't breathe.

I don't hear what else they say. I don't wait for Chase to turn back around. I just take a step back, and then another, heart pounding so loud it drowns out everything else.

All I can think is… I knew it.

I knew it was too good to be true.

I push through the front doors like the air inside was choking me.

The night hits sharp and cold, cab horns echo from the street, and headlights streak past. My heels click against the pavement as I stalk to the curb, one arm outstretched, trying to hail a taxi with shaking fingers.

It's New York, so they all keep driving.

"Scarlett—wait!"

His voice slices through the hum of the city, and I squeeze my eyes shut like that might keep the tears in. No such luck.

"Scarlett, stop—just let me talk to you."

I whirl around. He's already halfway to me, hair mussed, worry etched all over his face.

"Don't," I snap, voice raw. "Don't come out here and act like this is something we can just *talk* through."

His jaw clenches. "Please, just give me a second. I didn't want it to be like that. It *was* a stupid joke, but—"

"You knew," I cut in, pointing at him. "You placed some stupid bet with your teammates about me. And yet you pretended it was real between us. You let me walk in there thinking I was—" My voice breaks. "I *trusted* you."

He steps closer, hands up like he's calming a skittish animal. "It started before I even really knew you. These guys place bets about literally everything. It's juvenile, and it meant absolutely nothing. Tyler ran his mouth, and I should've shut it down. And I'm really sorry I didn't—"

"You're sorry?" I scoff, bitter and breathless.

"You don't get to make me question everything and then tell me it was just some silly game."

That lands. He flinches.

"Don't you dare gaslight me into thinking this is nothing." I wipe a very inconvenient tear from my cheek.

I don't wait for him to recover. Another cab comes rolling toward us, and this time, I step into the street without hesitation, arm out.

The driver slows, then stops. I throw the door open and climb in, wiping at my eyes as I give him the hotel's name.

Chase stands there on the sidewalk, helpless.

"Scarlett—please don't go like this."

I meet his eyes through the window.

"I already did."

The door shuts. The cab pulls away.

And I don't look back.

The hotel room is too nice for how miserable I feel.

Fluffy white duvet, marble bathroom, blackout curtains drawn tight. A tray of untouched room service sits on the table—something that was supposed to pass as dinner last night but ended up just being a sad reminder that I can't eat around a lump in my throat.

I haven't slept. Not really.

I spent most of the night curled in bed, knees to my chest, flipping between being furious and being wrecked and then hating myself for feeling either. My laptop's been open for hours, the screen glowing softly beside me in the tangle of sheets.

Strangely, I'm still able to write—with even more raw emotion than before.

My headphones are on, volume up so high it practically vibrates my skull—something angry and female—Billie Eilish? Ashe, maybe? I don't even remember adding them to my playlist, but they're perfect. Loud, raw, unapologetic.

I type and delete and retype the same scene over and over, tears dripping down my cheeks like my body's leaking feelings I don't know what to do with. I've ignored every call and text from Chase. Watched his name light up my screen over and over until I finally flipped my phone facedown and shoved it under a pillow.

Only one message gets through.

Lucy: *hey. please just tell me you're alive so I don't stage a manhunt.*

I wait five minutes. Then ten. Then sigh, grab the phone, and type out a response. I *am* in the middle of New York City. I don't want them to think I got lost or kidnapped.

Me: *Alive. Just not in the mood to be someone's bet tonight.*

I don't send anything else. When she replies with a string of heart emojis and a "let me know if you need anything," I shut the phone off completely. I don't need people trying to fix it. I don't even know what *it* is yet.

The team has a game tonight, and I said I'd be there.

But instead, I'm in an oversized hoodie and yesterday's eyeliner, curled on the hotel bed with a blanket over my head like a haunted little gremlin.

I flick the TV on.

The Stampede game is already in the second period.

And Chase... looks awful.

He's missing passes he usually nails in his sleep. Skating like his legs are made of wet sand. One of his shots sails so far wide it actually makes the announcer pause.

He's playing like shit.

Something curls low in my chest, hot and aching. I wrap the blanket tighter around me.

Good, I think at first. Let him feel like garbage too.

But then I watch him get slammed into the boards, and all that righteous fury flickers into something softer. Something worse.

Because for all the hurt, for all the betrayal... I still care.

And that might be the cruelest part of all.

33

THE BET, THE SILENCE, AND THE SCREW-UP

Chase

The locker room is quiet in that heavy, post-loss kind of way. A few guys are half-dressed, going through the motions—untaping sticks, peeling off gear like it's the only thing keeping them from exploding. No one's making eye contact.

I sit slumped on the bench, pads still on, sweat dripping down my neck. I haven't said a word since the final buzzer.

I don't hear most of what's going on around me—just the low murmur of pissed-off teammates.

I played like shit. Worse than shit. Like I had no business being on the ice.

And I know exactly why.

"Yo," Bennett says, dropping onto the bench across from me, arms resting on his knees like he's just settling in for a chat. "You gonna keep playing like your skates are made of cement, or are you gonna go fix the thing that's clearly breaking your brain?"

I don't even look at him. I just stare at the floor and wipe a hand down my face. "It's not that simple."

"It never is."

I let out a bitter breath. "I messed up."

"Yeah." He doesn't sugarcoat it. "You did."

I finally glance at him. "Thanks. Real comforting."

"I'm not here to comfort you," he says. "I'm here to tell you to stop being a dumbass."

That gets a flicker of something out of me. Barely.

He leans back against the lockers, eyes on mine. "I've seen the way you look at her. Like she's it for you."

I shake my head, throat tight. "Doesn't matter. I didn't tell her about the bet. I let it go on. I made her think she was some... game."

"And now you're punishing yourself for it instead of doing anything to fix it." He gives me a look. "Congrats, you're the brooding antihero in a sad indie movie."

I almost laugh, but it comes out hollow.

"You waiting around for her to just forgive you out of the blue?" Bennett asks. "Because that's not gonna happen. You gotta move, man. You gotta *do* something."

"She won't want to hear from me."

He shrugs. "Maybe. Maybe not. You won't know until you try."

That hits. Hard.

He stands and claps a hand on my shoulder. "Don't let your pride mess this up. Not if it matters."

He walks off, leaving me alone in the silence, my heart pounding like I'm still out on the ice.

Because it does matter.

It matters more than anything.

And I have no idea if she'll even read a message from me.

But I know one thing—I can't stay quiet anymore.

Back in my room, I sit on the edge of the bed, staring at my phone.

I've typed out three messages already and deleted them all.

The first one was too casual.

The second one was too long.

The third one just didn't hit right.

I don't know how to fix this.

I just know I want to.

Finally, I open a new message. My thumbs hover over the keyboard for a second, and then I just… let it out.

Me: *I don't have a good excuse.*

I should've told you about the bet the second the stupid words were out of Ty's mouth. Before you ever became real to me.

And you are. You're the most real thing in my life right now.

You were never a game. Not for one second.

I'm sorry I made you feel that way.

You don't have to forgive me.

But I needed you to know the truth.

All of it.

I stare at it for a long time.

No begging. No explaining. Just the truth.

I hit send before I can change my mind.

Then I toss my phone on the bed and run both hands through my hair, heart pounding like I just stepped off the ice again.

I don't expect her to respond.

But I hope she does.

I really hope she does.

34

OKAY FINE, I HAVE FEELINGS

Scarlett

Back in Dallas a couple of days later, the brunch spot Lucy picked is loud and hip. I'm not sure if I'm underdressed or over-dressed, and I honestly don't care—I'm just trying not to cry into my mimosa.

Lucy ordered pancakes the size of a pizza and slid half the stack onto my plate without asking. "You'll feel better after carbs," she said, like it's a universal law.

She's not wrong.

"I can't believe you didn't come to the game," she says now, twisting a straw wrapper between her fingers. "Bennett said Chase was off all night. Like, epically bad."

I stab a piece of pancake. "Yeah, well."

She watches me. "You talk to him?"

"No." I shove the bite in my mouth and immediately regret it—it's too sweet and I have a lump in my throat the size of Texas, and now I have to swallow this.

Lucy doesn't say anything. She just refills my mimosa and pulls her phone out to scroll, giving me space without disappearing. It's the exact right move, which somehow makes me want to cry more.

I glance at my phone for the first time all day.

1 unread message from Chase Remington.

I freeze. I haven't read through all his messages—haven't wanted to.

My heart does that awful stutter-jump thing it always does around his name. Like it hasn't figured out he broke it yet.

I stare at the screen for a long time before opening it.

Chase: *I don't have a good excuse.*

I should've told you about the bet the second the stupid words were out of Ty's mouth. Before you ever became real to me.

And you are. You're the most real thing in my life right now.

You were never a game. Not for one second.

I'm sorry I made you feel that way.

You don't have to forgive me.

But I needed you to know the truth.

All of it.

My throat tightens.

I blink down at the screen, trying to breathe through the ache in my chest.

Lucy leans over to peek. "Is that…?"

I nod, not trusting my voice.

She reads it quietly, then sits back, giving me a soft look. "Okay, I know I said I was team 'throw him off a cliff,' but… that's a pretty damn good apology."

I press the phone to my chest and stare out the window, lips trembling.

"I don't know if it changes anything," I say finally.

"No," she agrees. "But it's a start."

And the worst part is… it feels like a start.

And that might be even scarier than if it didn't.

When I get home, I immediately call Harper.

She answers on the second ring, chipper and oblivious. "Heyyy, what's up, book slut?"

I exhale a laugh, my first real one all day. "I missed you."

"You sound emotionally wrecked. Should I be flattered or concerned?"

"Both."

I shift onto my side, one leg tangled in the sheets. "Something happened."

"Talk to me."

So I do. I tell her everything—how I overheard the guys at dinner talking about the bet, how I left, how Chase chased me down (no pun intended), how I've been ignoring him for a full two days like I'm starring in my own personal soap opera.

I tell her about the message he sent. How it gutted me in a way I didn't expect. How I can't stop thinking about the look on his face when I slammed that cab door.

When I finish, there's a long pause.

And then Harper says, "Soooo... do you want me to say 'I told you so,' or remind you of our bet?"

Our bet?

I start remembering bits and pieces of a conversation we had after getting pedicures last month. And my stomach drops.

"If you did fall for him, I'd never let you live it down." Harper had chuckled at my obvious discomfort.

I'd narrow my eyes. "Is that a bet?"

"More like a prophecy. But sure. Let's call it a bet. I say by the end of this book club fiasco, you're going to catch real feelings for Chase Remington."

Alarm bells ring in my brain.

"Oh my gosh," I gasp.

"Ding ding ding," she says sweetly. "Full circle, babe."

I cover my face with one hand. "I'm the worst."

"You're a human. With feelings. Who maybe, possibly, might've caught some for the hot hockey player she swore she hated."

"I placed a bet on falling in love. And then got mad that he—" I groan into the pillow. "I'm the world's biggest hypocrite."

"Yeah," she says gently, "but at least you're a cute one."

I smile weakly. "You're not mad at me?"

"Mad? Babe, I'm delighted. This is peak romance novel irony. I might throw a parade."

I roll onto my back, the weight of it all still there—but lighter now. Like letting someone else hold part of it made it bearable.

"Why don't you admit what this really is?"

I stare at the wall. "And what's that?"

"You fell for him, and that scared you."

The weight of her words slams into me.

There's a small chance she's right. Tiny. Minuscule.

Crap.

Harper lowers her voice. "So… what are you gonna do?"

I stare at my phone a second longer.

Then I open a new message. My fingers don't even hesitate.

I'd spent so long building walls that I forgot to leave a door. Chase didn't knock—he just moved in through the window. And now he was rearranging all my carefully organized defenses, making himself at home in places I'd sworn no one would ever reach again.

Me: *I think I'm ready to talk.*

I hit send.
He replies immediately.

Chase: *Yeah? Let's do it.*

Me: *But first I need to go to Chicago.*

My heart stutters.
And for the first time in two days, I let myself hope.

Chase: *Okay. I'll be here when you get back.*

I've had this idea in my head for months, well, years if I'm being honest, but I always talked myself out of it. Now, it feels like a bad idea. Like colossally bad.

The kind of bad idea you only follow through on after a dramatic therapy session or a staged intervention. Except this time, I've got neither. Just a slowly healing heart, a half-finished manuscript, and the urge to stop letting the past drive the car.

So I've flown to Chicago.
And texted my parents separately.
Dinner. Giordano's. 7 p.m. Be civil or be gone.

Short. Sharp. Me.

Now they're here.

And I actually have to do the thing.

My mom's sitting on the left side of the table, hands folded in front of her like she's trying to appear unbothered. My dad's on the right, arms folded, glancing occasionally at his phone like he's hoping someone will emergency-text him out of the restaurant.

Spoiler: no one is.

I'm sitting in front of them, a wine glass in one hand, not drinking it.

"I didn't invite you here to referee," I say finally. "I'm not interested in watching you two volley passive-aggressive barbs across the table."

My mom straightens. "Scarlett, we're not—"

"You are. You always have."

My dad sighs but doesn't argue. That's how I know he knows I'm right.

"I'm thirty," I say. "I write about love for a living. I think about it constantly. And I still have no idea what it's supposed to look like. Because growing up? It looked like slammed doors and stony silence and one of you always walking out."

They both look at me now. Really look.

"I didn't get a normal childhood," I say. "And I've spent most of my adult life convincing myself that love is temporary. Transactional. That people only stay if you make it easy. Or if you happen to live inside of a Nicholas Sparks novel."

My mom's eyes are glistening. My dad's jaw is tight. The tension between us is as thick as ever.

"I'm not blaming you," I add quickly. "Okay, well—I am, a little. But mostly I just... I need something from you."

They wait.

I take a breath, try to steady myself.

"I need you to tell me what happened. I need you to be honest with me. Because for once, I think I want my own happy ending, and all I hear is you two tearing each other down in the background."

Silence. Thick. Uncomfortable.

And then—

"We were stupid," my dad says.

My mom blinks. "Excuse me?"

Here we go...

He turns toward her, voice low but clear. "We were stubborn. We were young. We thought love would fix things, but we didn't know how to talk. How to fight for each other."

"We fought plenty," she mutters.

"Not for the *right* things."

I watch them—two people who once built a life together, now looking at each other like strangers who might've once shared a dream.

"I didn't leave because I stopped loving you," he says. "I left because I didn't know how to stay."

"And I didn't stop you," my mom admits. "I

was so tired of feeling like the only one trying."

Tears slip down my cheeks before I even feel them coming.

They both look at me.

"I'm sorry," my mom says. "I didn't realize how much you were carrying."

"I thought staying quiet would protect you," my dad adds. "But it just made you feel like none of it mattered."

I nod, not trusting my voice.

I just sit there.

Right between them.

It's quiet again.

Nothing is fixed, and it might not ever be, but something tells me it's a start.

We eat, share a bottle of wine, and we talk some more. And somehow, by the end of dinner, I feel the tiniest bit better. My parents are just people— flawed humans who made mistakes.

The three of us step out onto the sidewalk. My mom hugs me first—tighter than she has in a long time.

"I'm sorry it took this long," she murmurs.

"Me too," I say, and I mean it.

My dad lingers a beat longer, like he's not sure he's earned the right to say anything else. But then he reaches for my hand and squeezes it.

"You deserved better," he says. "And I'm going to try. Even now. If you'll let me."

I nod, throat tight. "Trying's a good place to start."

They head in opposite directions, but this time, it doesn't feel like something's breaking apart.

It feels like turning a page. Starting a new chapter.

And maybe that's enough for now.

35

PIZZA, APOLOGIES, AND OTHER UN-EXPECTED THINGS

Scarlett

He said to meet him on the rooftop.

Of course he did. He probably thought it sounded romantic. Poetic. Like something out of a slow-burn Netflix drama where the girl forgives the guy with a dramatic kiss and a fade to black.

Joke's on him—I'm wearing sneakers and anxiety.

The rooftop is quiet when I push the door open. Windy. A little too cinematic, if I'm honest. String lights zigzag above a few lounge chairs, and the skyline stretches out in front of us like it knows we're about to have *a moment*.

Chase is standing near the edge, hands in his

pockets, staring out at the city like he's been up here practicing what to say.

He turns when he hears me. Doesn't smile. Just watches me walk toward him, as if he's not sure I won't decide to run.

Truthfully, I'm not either.

"Hey," I say, because I'm great at grand entrances.

"Hey."

We stand there for a beat. Two. I fold my arms to keep from fidgeting.

"Kind of dramatic, don't you think?" I nod at the skyline. "What, no rooftop string quartet?"

He huffs out a laugh. It sounds like it hurts.

"Thought I'd keep it low-key."

"Well, nothing says casual like emotional trauma and mood lighting."

He nods, lips pressed together, eyes scanning mine as if he's trying to read what I'm thinking.

"I didn't know if I was going to come," I say.

"I didn't know if you would either."

I blink. "Wow. Off to a strong start."

He winces. "That's not what I—look, I meant… I wouldn't have blamed you if you didn't. But I'm glad you did."

Silence stretches between us again. The wind tugs at my hair. It smells like the city up here, and maybe rain and something else I can't name.

"I was humiliated," I say finally. "Standing there, hearing them talk about me like I was some… experiment. A bet with a deadline."

His face twists like the words physically hurt him.

"I know," he says quietly. "You have every right to feel that way."

"I wasn't just mad," I add, staring past him at the skyline. "I was embarrassed. I *finally* let my guard down and let someone in, and it turns out the universe was laughing at me."

"Scarlett—"

"I know you didn't plan it. But you knew. And you didn't tell me."

"I didn't want to ruin what we were building; it felt so fragile..."

"Yeah, well." I shrug.

That hangs there like smoke.

He nods once, eyes locked on mine. "I should've told you. No excuse. But it was never a joke to me. You weren't a stunt, or a bet, or part of the PR campaign. You were *you*. And I was already gone."

I exhale slowly. Might as well rip the band-aid off. "That would be more touching if I didn't feel like a moron for making a bet of my own."

He blinks. "Wait… what?"

"Yeah." I rub my eyes. "Harper and I—she bet me I'd fall for you."

His eyebrows lift, a small flicker of surprise on his face. "Details, please."

"Not to quote Shakespeare, but it was one of those 'the lady doth protest too much' situations. She thought all my venom toward you meant the opposite. Of course, at the time, I brushed her off, told her no way. But yeah, there was still a bet—at least on her end."

Chase looks surprised but doesn't say anything more.

"So I guess I'm a walking hypocrite," I add.

He takes a tentative step closer. "Maybe we're just two idiots who didn't see this coming."

I look up at him. He's beautiful. Calm, and rational. And that's *so annoying.*

He's literally the perfect male specimen—tall, roguishly handsome with scruff on his jaw and kind eyes…

"I'm still mad," I admit.

"Okay."

"I'm not ready to forgive you."

"Okay."

"But I'm tired of pretending I don't care."

Something shifts in his expression. It's soft and vulnerable and stupidly earnest.

"You don't have to fall," he says. "Just lean. I'll catch you."

My heart stumbles. I don't move for a second. Just stare at him like he might evaporate if I blink too hard.

Then, slowly, I step forward.

I press my forehead against his chest.

He doesn't say anything. He just wraps his arms around me and lets me just *be*, lets me breathe him in. And it feels… safe. For the first time in a while.

It's not fixed.

It's not perfect.

But it's *real*.

"I know you're scared, Scar. I get it. But believe me, I'm not going anywhere."

His words are a sweet balm to my tattered heart. And they do help—just the tiniest bit.

Eventually, I pull back just enough to breathe, and Chase looks at me like I just handed him his heart back, his gaze full of admiration and something warm.

He touches my cheek with his thumb.

I lean into his touch, my voice barely above a whisper. "I don't need you."

His face changes, something flickering in his eyes—hurt, maybe, or disappointment.

"But I want you," I continue, meeting his gaze. "And that's so much scarier."

His breath catches. "Scarlett…"

"Needing someone means you're incomplete without them. But wanting someone when you're already whole? When you've already proven you can do it alone?" I swallow hard. "That's choosing to hand them the power to wreck you, even when you don't have to."

"Never gonna wreck you, baby." He gazes at me with those eyes that see way too much, and I'm lost.

Then he clears his throat. "So, uh… I was gonna ask if you were hungry."

"I could eat. What did you have in mind?"

He grins. "Pizza?"

I smile. "Only if I get full veto power on toppings."

"Oh, absolutely not," he says as we start toward the stairs. "This is a democracy."

"It is *not* a democracy. You eat pineapple on pizza."

"Because I'm a man of culture."

"You're what's wrong with America."

He laughs, and it's this warm, surprised thing that makes my chest do something deeply inconvenient.

We walk a few blocks until we find a tiny hole-in-the-wall pizzeria with paper plates, checkered tables, and a neon sign that probably hasn't worked properly since 2003. In other words—perfect.

We order a pie half his way, half mine, because apparently we've reached *that* level of maturity, and slide into a corner booth like this is just… normal.

And honestly? It kind of is.

I sip my Pepsi and gaze over at him.

He leans back like he owns the place. And I

can't help but notice how cute he looks. Dark jeans. Black hoodie. Black hat turned backwards. "You know, if this were a date, I'd be crushing it right now."

I raise a brow. "Bringing a woman to a pizza place with questionable health grades and fluorescent lighting?"

He shrugs. "It's bold. Unexpected. Sexy in a working-class hero kind of way."

I smirk. "You really are unwell."

He grins at me, and for a second, I forget about everything else, because he really is that pretty.

And this feels good.

Normal. *Us*.

Our pizza is delivered to the table shockingly fast—my half is mushrooms, olives, and extra cheese—enough to kill a lactose-intolerant person. His is pineapple, pepperoni, and jalapeños. Sweet and spicy—a lot like him.

"Feel free to have a slice of mine," he says, sliding a piece of pie onto his paper plate. "I might just expand your palate."

"You'll expand my rage." I grin sweetly.

"How was Chicago?" he asks.

"Good," I say quickly. "I had a sit-down chat with both of my parents in the same room for the first time in decades."

His eyebrows lift. "And?"

I swallow. "And it was good, healing in a way.

Probably sounds stupid how much I let them affect me for so long."

He touches my hand. "Just because someone carries it well doesn't mean the weight isn't heavy."

I release a slow breath and realize he's right. I don't have to carry the weight of my parents' failures anymore. It's time to choose me—my life.

"So," he says between bites, "most embarrassing moment. Go."

I blink at him. "That's a very personal first-date question."

"This is technically our eighth public outing."

I fake-count on my fingers. "Does that include the time I heckled you in front of thousands of fans?"

"Especially that one."

I sigh dramatically. "Fine. But if you ever tell anyone, I will burn your house down."

"I can accept those terms."

I lean back, arms crossed. "Senior year, I tripped during a pep rally in front of the entire school. And fell face-first into the tuba section. My skirt went up. It was… not a good day."

He chokes on his soda. "Into the *tuba section*?"

"I was airborne. There was *altitude*."

He's doubled over now, laughing so hard he's turning red.

I throw a balled-up napkin at his head. "Your turn, jackass."

He wipes his eyes. "Okay, okay. Mine's bad."

"Worse than flying into brass instruments while showing your underwear?"

"Debatable. Rookie year, locker room prank war got out of hand. Someone swapped my shampoo for Nair."

My jaw drops. "No."

"Oh yeah. I lost half an eyebrow and a decent chunk of my pride."

I'm wheezing now. "Did you play like that?"

"Yup. There's footage. The internet is forever."

I'm laughing so hard I nearly drop my slice. He's grinning at me like he can't believe this is real, and maybe I can't either.

Because somehow, even after everything, it's *easy* again. The kind of easy you don't fake. The kind you fall into without meaning to. Like we've been doing this for years.

I look at him—really look at him—and the warmth in my chest isn't just about pizza or banter or tuba-based trauma.

It's him.

Still him.

Maybe always him.

36

THIRD WHEEL WITH PAWS

Chase

I don't want the night to end. That's all I can think about as I watch Scarlett across the table.

She's smiling, debating another slice of pizza, and I'm dangerously close to convincing myself I haven't completely wrecked things between us.

We've been bickering for over an hour—about pizza toppings, about which Ninja Turtle has the best energy (it's obviously Raphael), about how I fold my pizza like a tourist—and somehow, it's perfect. Easy. Familiar.

She wipes her hands on a napkin and leans back, stretching. "Alright. That hit the spot. My heart's still broken, but at least I'm full."

I grin. "That's all I've ever wanted to hear from a woman."

She rolls her eyes, but she's not pushing away anymore. Not like before.

I take a breath. "You wanna come over?"

Her brows lift slightly. "Subtle."

I fight off a laugh because *of course* she calls me on my terrible line. But instead of backing down, I lean into it. "It's late. We're both riding the high of surviving pineapple pizza trauma."

She doesn't say anything, so I go for the real hook.

"Plus, Rip misses you."

That gets her.

"Oh, *Rip* misses me?"

I nod solemnly. "Hasn't stopped whining since you left. Practically watched *The Notebook* without me last night."

She smirks, but there's something warm in her eyes now. "Yeah, I wouldn't want to deprive your emotionally needy dog."

"So that's a yes?"

She shrugs, but it's playful. "Let's go before I remember I'm supposed to be mad at you."

I try not to smile as we slide out of the booth.

My place is dark when we enter, and I immediately hear the soft jingle of Rip's collar as he trots out to greet her like she's been gone for a year.

I flip on the kitchen light.

"Wow," she says, crouching to scratch behind his ears. "There's my best guy."

"Honestly, I'm the third wheel in this relationship," I mutter, locking the door behind us.

She toes off her shoes and pads into the living room like she's done it a dozen times—which she hasn't, but it feels like she has.

"You want anything to drink?"

She shakes her head. "I'm good."

"I feel like it's a movie-in-bed kind of night. You in?"

She gives me a look. "Are you trying to get me into your bed, Remington?"

"Is it working?"

Rip—*my man*—leads the way, tail wagging, and Scarlett follows.

She's never seen my bedroom, and she pauses in the doorway.

She doesn't say much at first; she just looks around. The walls are painted a soft gray, and there's a worn leather chair in the corner. The king-sized bed is halfway made—the dark gray duvet flung haphazardly over the mattress. If she notices I sleep like a human tornado, she doesn't call me on it. One pillow's near the foot, another is sideways by the headboard.

Her eyes linger on the photo by the window, the one of me and my brother on the frozen pond back home. Then they land on the book by the nightstand. *Her* book.

Finally, she sits on the side of the bed. "I expected more trophies. Or at least one life-sized cutout of yourself."

I grin. "That's in storage."

Scarlett laughs, and it's the best sound in the world.

I queue up some random comfort movie—something we'll pretend to watch and absolutely won't. We end up propped against pillows, the flatscreen streaming some chaotic rom-com neither of us is paying attention to. Rip is at our feet like he's supervising.

I look at her then—really look—and she's close, warm, soft around the edges in a way that makes my chest ache. Her lips are right there. Her sarcasm is right there. And I want all of it.

So I lean in slowly, giving her time to pull away. She doesn't.

Our mouths meet in that soft, tentative way that says *this is new again, but it's still us.*

She shifts closer, hand sliding up my chest, and suddenly it's not tentative anymore.

It's heat and memory and want. It's her fingers in my hair and my hands on her waist and the soft sound she makes when I deepen the kiss like I've been dying to.

Rip sighs at our feet like he's unimpressed. We

ignore him.

We kiss until we forget there was ever a reason not to.

We eventually pull apart, breathless and dazed, her forehead resting against mine.

Neither of us speaks right away.

She's still close—so close—and all I can think is *don't screw this up again.*

She blinks at me, lips pink and kiss-bruised. "So… are we still watching this movie, or are we just lying to Rip now?"

I glance at the screen where two characters are having an aggressively slow-motion food fight. "I think even Rip has checked out."

Scarlett turns her head, and sure enough, he's passed out at the foot of the bed, paws twitching in some epic dog dream.

She shifts again, curling on her side to face me. "Okay, full honesty."

"Hit me."

"I'm terrified."

That knocks something loose in my chest. I meet her eyes. "Of what?"

"Of how easy this feels," she says softly. "Like I should still be mad at you. Like I shouldn't… trust this again. But I do. And that makes me feel like a walking red flag."

I reach for her hand, thread my fingers through hers.

"I'm scared too," I admit. "I don't know what this is supposed to look like. But I know I want to find out. With you."

She lets out a shaky breath, then mutters, "You're really hot when you're sincere."

I grin. "Don't tell anyone. I've got a reputation to protect."

She settles in closer, head on my chest, like it's the most natural thing in the world.

We lie there in the quiet, her fingers tracing lazy lines across my ribs, my hand wrapped around her waist.

And for the first time in a long time, my brain shuts up.

No noise. No second-guessing. Just this.

Her.

Us.

I press a kiss to the top of her head.

She murmurs something I almost don't catch. "If I fall asleep here, you're not allowed to say 'I told you so.'"

"Wouldn't dream of it."

But I do smile to myself in the dark and hold her a little tighter.

Because she's here.

Because she stayed.

37

THAT'S MY GIRL

Chase

NINE MONTHS LATER

She walks into the bookstore like she owns the place.

And, well—tonight, she kind of does.

Scarlett's in this deep green dress that hugs her in all the right places, hair pulled back, smile wide but slightly nervous in a way only I'd notice. The crowd erupts the second she appears—readers, bloggers, publishing people, book club members in matching T-shirts that say *I Read Romance and Tackle People Who Don't.*

Man, she's ridiculous.

And completely incredible.

She spots me through the crowd—standing by the back table, hands in my pockets, playing it cool even though my heart's doing something dumb and teenage—and her face softens just a little.

Like I'm the thing she was looking for.

She makes her way through the crowd, stopping to take selfies with fans, sign books, and chat. I can't take my eyes off her.

When she stops beside me, I lean down and press a quick kiss to her mouth. "You good?"

She nods, somewhat dazed. "I can't believe this many people showed up."

"You shouldn't be surprised. You wrote something real."

She glances at me, eyes bright but wary. "You practicing for your acceptance speech as boyfriend of the year?"

"Nah," I say, wrapping an arm around her waist. "That one's for the after-party."

She laughs—really laughs—and I swear I'd walk through fire to hear that sound on loop for the rest of my life.

From the front of the store, someone taps a mic and calls her name. She groans. "That's my cue to make a heartfelt speech and pretend I'm not internally screaming."

I give her hand a squeeze. "Go melt hearts, Calloway. And afterward, I'm taking you home to celebrate."

She leans up, presses a quick kiss to my cheek, and whispers, "I can hardly wait."

She pulls away and heads toward the crowd, shoulders back, chin high. I watch her go, full of pride and something deeper—something quieter and heavier and terrifying in the best way.

Because nine months ago, I wasn't sure if I'd ever get to see this.

Scarlett steps up to the little mic stand near the front of the store, framed by a wall of her books and a blown-up cover poster with her name in big, gold foil letters. The crowd hushes, buzzing with the kind of giddy energy I've only ever felt in packed arenas before the puck drops.

She clears her throat, tapping the mic once. "Okay. Hi. Wow."

The crowd laughs, and she gives them a sheepish smile that does something inconvenient to my heart.

"So… I had this whole speech planned," she says, glancing down at a folded index card in her hand, "but then I realized it made me sound like a robot who swallowed a thesaurus, so I'm just gonna wing it."

More laughter. Someone from the book club yells, "We love chaos!"

"This book was hard to write," she continues, her voice a little steadier now. "Like, rip-your-hair-out, stare-at-the-ceiling, ugly-cry-in-the-bathroom hard. I thought I'd lost my voice. I thought I was done."

She pauses, glancing toward the back—toward *me*.

"But someone reminded me that stories don't have to be perfect to matter. That sometimes the best ones are a little messy, a little bruised. That love doesn't always show up on schedule, but when it does… it's worth writing about."

My chest tightens. The room goes quiet in that reverent, leaning-in way.

"So, thank you," she finishes, looking out at the crowd. "For being here. For reading. For letting me be messy, and loud, and wildly romantic about things I swore I'd given up on."

A pause.

"And thank you to the guy in the back who made me pancakes when I couldn't get out of bed, and who buys every edition of my book just to make it look like I'm popular."

Everyone turns to look at me, and I swear my ears turn red.

Scarlett grins. "This one's for you."

Applause breaks out—loud and warm and full of love.

She steps down from the mic and disappears into a sea of hugs and compliments, and all I can do is watch her, completely and hopelessly gone.

38

AUTHOR BY DAY, HOT MESS BY NIGHT

Scarlett

The bar is loud, full, and very, *very* into me right now, which is weird.

I'm not great at being the center of attention, and I doubt I ever will be.

The moment I walk in, Harper shoves a cocktail into my hand and yells, "She wrote a BOOK!" to the entire room, as if she's announcing a baby's gender.

Chase's teammates are gathered at the back booth, all towering, loud, and already halfway tipsy. Bennett waves at me with both arms like he's guiding a plane. Lucy is beside him, sipping something pink with a sugared rim, looking unbothered by the chaos.

"Scottie!" Harper shouts, dragging me toward the bar as if I'm not wearing heels and four hours of emotional vulnerability. "You did it! You made me cry! And you didn't even kill anyone in this one!"

"High praise," I say, grinning.

She turns to the bartender. "Two tequila shots, author's tab!"

"Wait—" I start to protest.

"Nope," she says. "You published a book and emotionally ruined me. This is happening."

The bartender sets down two shot glasses, and for once, I don't argue with Harper. I put her through a lot while writing this book. My publisher canceled my contract when I switched genres, but Harper fought for me. She found a new home for my book and negotiated an even better deal. We've been through hell together and come out on the other side. It's worth celebrating.

The tequila burns, but in a warm, victorious way.

I navigate through the bar, dodging congratulations and compliments. Chase appears behind me like a warm shadow, slipping an arm around my waist.

"You surviving your own party?" he murmurs, his lips brushing my temple.

"Barely. If one more person asks if the male lead is based on a real person, I might launch myself into traffic."

He grins. "Is he?"

I shoot him a look. "You wish, Remington."

We settle into the corner booth with his team-mates, who are trying to outdo each other with dramatic readings of my book. Tyler has one hand on his chest, reciting a steamy scene like it's Shakespeare. Will is fake-swooning. Bennett is crying into a pint of beer.

"Can we not?" I mutter, burying my face in Chase's shoulder.

"I tried to stop them," he says, not even pretending to sound sincere.

Harper slides in beside me, stealing a fry off someone's plate. "They're idiots. But hot idiots. You should put them in your next book."

I sip my drink. "Oh, I'm already mentally killing them off in book two."

She grins. "There she is."

Somewhere between round three of drinks and Chase feeding me a mozzarella stick like I'm royalty, I realize something strange.

I feel… okay.

Happy, even.

It's loud and chaotic, and I'm being lovingly harassed by athletes with zero boundaries, but I feel *good*. Like I earned this. Like I deserve to be celebrated.

Chase catches me looking at him.

"What?" he asks.

I shake my head, smiling. "Nothing."

But what I really mean is: *Everything.*

By the time we leave the bar, I'm buzzed on tequila, compliments, and the terrifying realization that I might be happy.

Chase wraps an arm around my shoulders as we walk toward his car, the night warm and quiet around us. My heels dangle from my fingers because my feet gave up two hours ago.

I yawn as he drives us home, tired but content.

He unlocks the door, and before I can step inside, a familiar thump-thump-thump of paws barrels down the hallway.

"Rip!" I drop my shoes and immediately crouch, greeted by the world's most dramatic dog, tail wagging as if he's been personally wronged by my absence. "Hi, baby," I say, scratching behind his ears. "Did you miss me? Did Dad tell you I published my book?"

Rip whines and licks my cheek, proud yet slightly offended he wasn't invited to the launch party.

I laugh, standing slowly, and Rip follows me like a shadow as I drift toward the living room. Chase disappears into the kitchen to grab us water, and I flop onto the couch, feeling the weight of the night settle over me—but in a good way. In a *I-did-the-thing-and-the-world-didn't-end* way.

He returns a minute later, hands me a glass, then slides in next to me, close enough that our legs press together.

"I'm proud of you," he says quietly.

I look over at him. "I know."

He huffs a laugh. "You're supposed to say 'thank you.'"

"Yeah, well. I'm still recovering from watching your friends do dramatic readings of my sex scenes."

He groans. "I will never be able to look Tyler in the eye again."

"Good. That makes two of us."

I take a sip of water and glance down at Rip, curled up at our feet like he knows this is a big moment and he's not about to ruin it.

Then I feel Chase's hand brush mine again. Not urgent. Not needy. Just there.

"I love you."

My heart skips.

He says it like it's not some grand declaration. Like it's the most obvious truth in the world.

"I know," I say, biting back a smile.

I lean in and kiss him—slow, soft, and grateful. His hands find my waist, grounding me.

"I love you too," I whisper.

Rip lets out a sigh from the floor.

I glance down. "Yeah, yeah. You were right all along."

Chase grins. "He totally called it."

We stay like that for a while—pressed together

on the couch, our dog-shaped third wheel asleep at our feet, everything finally still.

And for the first time in forever, the ending doesn't scare me.

Because this?

This feels like a beginning.

39

BETTER THAN FICTION

Scarlett

I didn't want an engagement party.

I said it multiple times. Loudly. In writing. Possibly even in all caps.

Harper ignored me, obviously.

Which is how I've ended up in Chase's backyard—correction, *our* backyard—surrounded by twinkling lights, overfed athletes, and roughly thirty people shouting, "Kiss! Kiss!" every time we stand within three feet of each other.

Rip is wearing a bow tie. It's clip-on. He looks thrilled.

"You doing okay?" Chase asks, slipping his arm around my waist as I rescue my third mini cupcake from a dangerously wobbly tower.

"Define okay."

He grins. "Are you going to bolt before Harper

gives her toast?"

"Unclear. She's had two margaritas, and I saw her holding a microphone earlier. It's not looking good."

Chase's family is here—his parents, Evie, and even Owen. My own parents are here too—tolerating each other. *Weird.*

Just then, Harper clinks a glass with a fork, and every molecule in my body prepares for flight.

"Everyone!" she shouts, swaying slightly in heels she *definitely* can't walk in. "I just want to say a few words before I black out!"

The crowd cheers like she's a rock star. I drop my head into Chase's chest.

"Kill me now," I whisper.

"You love this."

"I love *you.* I tolerate this."

Harper winks at me from across the yard. "I've known Scarlett since college, and I can say with full confidence that she is terrifying, *brilliant*, allergic to vulnerability, and definitely did *not* believe in love until this man over here"—she points wildly at Chase—"broke through her cold little heart like an emotionally intelligent linebacker."

I choke on my champagne.

Everyone cheers.

Traitors.

Chase chuckles under his breath and pulls me tighter, kissing the top of my head.

Harper keeps going. "I knew they were end-game when her writing changed. One day, it went from I-can-do-it-all-on-my-own to learning how to let someone in. That was the moment I realized she was done for. Her editor probably knew before we all did."

The crowd erupts with laughter. Chase is full-on *shaking* with silent laughter beside me. I'm going to die. This is how I go.

Prepare my casket now.

I've heard you can get one at Costco nowadays.

Harper holds up her glass. "To Scarlett and Chase—may your love be big, messy, book-worthy, and full of snacks. I love you both. Please don't divorce each other unless it's for a *really* good plot twist."

Everyone cheers. I wipe at my eyes, attributing it to the wind. Or allergies. Or the fact that I somehow found the exact person I didn't think existed, and now I get to marry him.

Chase turns to me, eyes soft and warm, as if the world has shrunk down to just this moment.

"You really love me," he murmurs.

"Unfortunately."

"Tragically."

He kisses me, and the crowd erupts in full rom-com-level applause.

Rip barks once, as if giving his blessing.

And just like that, I stop caring about speeches

or parties or anything else.

Because this? This is my definition of perfect.

Bennett strolls up, clapping Chase on the back to congratulate him. "Are you crying?" he asks.

Chase wipes his cheek. "No. I got something in my eye."

Bennett grins. "Yeah, it's called a tear."

Chase gives him a firm look. "Must be allergies."

I snuggle into his side even more. My own personal hockey-playing teddy bear. He's a total softie. And I love him completely.

Gag, I know.

Later, there are tacos and cake and drunken speeches by more of our friends. But then it's just me and Chase getting ready for bed, and I'm happier than I've ever been.

The house is quiet. We bought a place together a few months ago—enough space for Rip to roam, and possibly even for babies, though the jury's still out on that one. I love our life as it is, so we'll see. We're in no rush.

I'm standing in our bedroom, still wearing the dress Harper made me buy, staring at my reflection in the mirror and trying to process the fact that I'm engaged. To a man who makes me laugh, makes me feel safe, and knows when to argue with me and when to just… hold my hand.

The door creaks open, and I see him in the mirror—leaning against the frame, tie undone, shirt sleeves rolled up.

"You look like a dream," he says, soft and low.

I smile. "That's just the champagne talking."

He walks over and wraps his arms around me from behind. His hands settle on my waist like they belong there. Like they always have.

"I didn't drink that much," he says into my neck. "You've always looked like this to me."

I turn slowly in his arms. "Like what?"

He brushes a strand of hair behind my ear. "Like the rest of my life."

I should make a joke. Deflect. Run my usual playbook. But I don't.

Because tonight, I just want to feel it.

"You're sappy when you're in love," I murmur, fingertips skimming the back of his neck.

"I'm sappy because I'm in love with *you.*"

He kisses me, gentle and lingering, like we have all the time in the world—and maybe we do now.

I let him walk me back toward the bed, the dress slipping over my shoulders and puddling to the floor like it knows its work here is done. He looks at me like I'm his whole world. It's a little overwhelming.

"I still can't believe you said yes," he says, his voice thick with wonder.

"I still can't believe you asked," I whisper back.

"Are you happy?"

His forehead rests against mine. I nod, my eyes stinging.

"I didn't think I could be. Not like this."

He kisses me again, and it's everything—soft, slow. Like he's memorizing every part of me he already knows by heart.

We move together like we've done this a hundred times but still want to savor it like the first. His touch is reverent, his words quiet and constant— *You're beautiful... I've got you... You're mine...*

Afterward, we drift off to sleep, limbs still tangled, fingers still linked. I think—

This is it.

This is what all the books tried to explain.

And for the first time in my life, I don't need to write the ending.

Because I'm already living it.

40

THE WEDDING

Scarlett

I always thought that if I got married, I'd elope. Courthouse, black dress, maybe a bouquet of snacks.

But standing here—barefoot in the grass under a canopy of string lights, holding hands with the man who once called romance novels "training manuals," while Rip trots down the aisle—I don't want to be anywhere else.

It's perfect.

Messy, loud, *our* kind of perfect.

Harper's crying into Lucy's shoulder. Bennett is holding the rings and looks more nervous than we do. Chase's teammates fill two rows, all massive and oddly emotional. My parents are here too—seated together, talking softly. That alone feels like a miracle.

And then there's Chase.

Captain of the Dallas Stampede.

The guy who once bribed a bookstore to re-stock my novel.

The man who kissed me like a promise and then *kept it.*

And somehow, impossibly, he's mine.

The officiant is saying something—something about partnership and patience and always putting the toilet seat down—but I'm not really listening.

Because Chase is looking at me like I'm his whole world. And I'm looking at him like he's mine.

When it's time to say our vows, he goes first.

"I knew I loved you the second you threatened to throw a latte at me," he says, and everyone laughs. "You were chaos wrapped in sarcasm, and I couldn't look away."

I roll my eyes through a tear.

"You've made me better," he says, his voice thick. "Not perfect. Just… *real.* You challenge me. Steady me. And every time I look at you, I'm reminded that I don't want to face this world without you next to me, preferably while yelling at a referee."

Laughter erupts again, and now I'm crying. Awesome.

"My vow," he finishes, "is that I'll show up. For all of it. For you. For us. Always."

I sniff once. Twice. Then clear my throat.

"My turn."

Chase smiles and waits.

"I used to think love was a trick ending," I say. "Something that looked pretty on paper but always fell apart in real life. But then you showed up. With confidence, with swagger, with a stupidly good jawline and a dog I'm pretty sure loves me more than you do."

Rip barks softly, and the crowd loses it.

"You didn't save me," I say. "You *saw* me. You made space for me. And then you stayed, even when I tried to push you away with every defense mechanism in the book."

I reach for his hand. "So here's mine… I'll keep showing up too. I'll write every chapter with you, even the hard ones."

A pause.

"And I'll try really hard not to kill you if you leave laundry on the floor."

He laughs, his eyes bright. "Fair."

We kiss. Someone cheers. Rip spins in a circle like he knows it's official.

And just like that, we're married.

I thought I'd feel scared—instead, I feel settled. Happy.

Ugh, I'm probably one of those people now.

Whatever. Hashtag—worth it!

41

FROM FACE-OFFS TO FOREVER

Chase

I'm standing in the kitchen wearing nothing but boxers, holding a spatula like a weapon and staring down a very burnt pancake.

Rip is judging me from the corner, lying dramatically across the floor as if he can't believe he's still living in these conditions.

"Don't look at me like that," I mutter. "She left me unsupervised."

From the bedroom, Scarlett's voice floats down the hall. "I can *smell* the failure."

"Bold words for someone who tripped over her own shoe while trying to chase down a UPS truck yesterday."

"I thought it was book mail!"

A second later, she appears in the doorway—hair wild, wearing one of my T-shirts and her pink slippers. She looks like chaos. She looks like home.

She peeks at the pan and winces. "Is that... carbon?"

"It was supposed to be breakfast."

"It looks like a crime scene."

I drop the spatula with a sigh. "You married me for my charm, not my culinary prowess."

She grins and walks over, wrapping her arms around my waist. "Good thing you're pretty."

We kiss, and it's easy and familiar. Rip groans from the floor as if we're embarrassing him again.

We honeymooned in Thailand.

We hosted our families for Thanksgiving, and no one yelled.

We made it through late nights, deadlines, road trips, sick days, and three lost socks to Rip's endless appetite.

And somehow, every version of us survived.

She slides her arms around my waist, resting her cheek against my chest.

"I like this," she says.

"What, my culinary downfall?"

"This," she murmurs, pressing closer.

I press a kiss to the top of her head. "I like it too."

And I do. More than I ever thought I could. Not just the big moments—though those have been good—but this.

Us.

She rests her cheek against my chest. "Can you believe it's been a year?"

"Depends," I say. "Are we counting the month when you considered divorcing me over the dog calendar?"

She gives me a look. "It was haunted, Chase."

"It was golden retrievers in Halloween costumes."

"The eyes *followed* me."

I shake my head, grinning. "Fine. But maybe you overreacted."

She snorts and pulls back to look up at me. "Okay, fine. Maybe I overreacted."

I raise a brow. "And maybe I undercooked our first Thanksgiving turkey by—"

"*Three hours,*" she finishes, smirking. "The fire alarm's still emotionally traumatized."

We both laugh, and it's the kind of laugh that carries a hundred tiny memories behind it.

She grabs her coffee off the counter, takes a sip, and says, "You know… one year ago today, we were in Thailand."

I nod. "No burnt pancakes there."

We both smile, remembering our honeymoon. We barely left the bed—which was fine by me.

I look at her—ridiculous pink slippers, brilliant, a little terrifying—and smile like an idiot.

Rip barks once, clearly demanding a second breakfast.

Scarlett sighs. "Okay, fine. Let's go out for pancakes. But *you're* cleaning that pan when we get home."

I press a kiss to her mouth. "Deal."

After getting dressed, we walk out the door—dog in tow, hand in hand, and one perfectly imperfect year down.

Forever to go.

EPILOGUE

FIVE YEARS LATER

Scarlett

"**R**ip, no—that's not food, that's Aunt Evie's baby!"

I lunge across my parents' living room, trying to intercept our golden retriever before he can lick Owen Jr.'s face for the thousandth time. The baby—Chase's nephew, officially the chunkiest, happiest six-month-old in existence—squeals with delight and grabs a fistful of Rip's ear.

"Some babysitters we are," Chase mutters, extracting dog fur from Owen's chubby fingers. "We've been here twenty minutes and already lost control."

"Speak for yourself," I say, then immediately trip over the diaper bag, sending both myself and its contents sprawling. "Okay, yeah, we're both disasters."

My mother watches from the kitchen doorway, trying and failing to hide her amusement. It's Thanksgiving again—our new tradition of actually spending holidays together instead of avoiding each other like the plague. Dad's in his usual chair, pretending to read the paper while obviously eavesdropping.

"You know," Mom says, bringing over a tray of coffee, "when you were Owen's age, you once ate half a houseplant while I was on a conference call."

"That explains so much," Chase says, earning himself an elbow to the ribs.

"I turned out fine," I protest, finally managing to separate dog from baby. Owen Jr. immediately starts crying about the loss of his fuzzy friend.

"You wrote three bestselling books about not needing anyone," Dad points out, lowering his newspaper. "Then married a hockey player and got a dog. 'Fine' is relative."

"And now I've written six romances," I counter. "The seventh comes out next month."

"Seven romance novels?" Mom blinks. "I thought you were on five."

"Time flies when you're writing happily ever afters," I say dryly, bouncing Owen on my hip.

He stops crying and starts blowing spit bubbles instead. "This one's got a single dad hockey player. I wonder where I got that inspiration."

Chase grins, reaching over to tickle Owen's

foot. "I better get royalties."

"You get dinner. Same thing."

"Your cooking has not improved in five years."

"Neither has yours," I shoot back.

My parents exchange a look—one of those weird, loaded glances that used to make me uncomfortable but now just makes me curious.

"What?" I ask, switching Owen to my other hip when he starts getting heavy.

Mom sets down her coffee cup, something soft in her expression. "It's just... you did it."

"Did what? Gained ten pounds from Chase's pancake obsession? Because yes, guilty."

"No." She shakes her head, smiling. "You proved us wrong. Both of us."

Dad clears his throat. "What your mother's trying to say is—we spent so many years showing you all the ways love could fail. How it could make you lose yourself. How it could break you."

"Super fun childhood memories," I mutter, but there's no heat in it anymore.

"But you found a way to have both," Mom continues. "Your independence, your career, your voice—and him." She nods at Chase, who's now making ridiculous faces at Owen. "You built something we couldn't."

"We're proud of you," Dad adds quietly. "For showing us it's possible."

I freeze, Owen now glued to my hip, because

my parents don't do this. We don't have Hallmark moments. We have sarcasm, carefully maintained boundaries, and the occasional shared meal where no one throws anything.

"I—" I start, then stop because my throat is doing that annoying tight thing.

Chase, because he's Chase and always knows when I need saving, swoops in and plucks Owen from my arms. "Good thing too, because I already put a deposit down on a puppy, so she's stuck with me."

"A WHAT?" I spin toward him.

He grins, all dimples and mischief. "Kidding. Mostly. Seventy-thirty kidding to not kidding."

"Chase Remington—"

"Sixty-forty?"

"We are *not* getting another dog!"

"Rip needs a friend," he protests, gesturing to where our dog has now sprawled across my mother's feet, demanding belly rubs. "Look how lonely he is."

"He's literally getting attention from three people right now."

"Four," Dad corrects, reaching down to scratch Rip's ear. "And I wouldn't mind a grandpuppy. Since actual grandchildren seem to be off the table."

"DAD."

Mom laughs—really laughs, the way she didn't

for so many years. "Leave them alone, Richard. They're young."

"I'm thirty-five," I remind her. "Chase is thirty-six. We're basically ancient."

"Ancient people who can't even babysit one infant without chaos," Chase adds, gesturing to Owen, who has somehow gotten yogurt in his hair despite us not giving him yogurt.

"Where did he even GET yogurt?" I ask.

Chase shrugs. "Babies are magic. Weird, sticky magic."

And standing there—in my parents' living room that used to be a battlefield, holding a yogurt-covered baby that isn't mine, arguing about hypothetical puppies with the man who was supposed to be everything I stood against—I realize something.

My parents were wrong about love making you lose yourself.

But they're right about one thing.

I did build something they couldn't.

I built a life where love doesn't mean sacrifice. Where independence doesn't mean loneliness. Where you can write romance novels about hockey players and still roast them in real life. Where your dog becomes everyone's grandchild, and your in-laws become actual family, and somehow, impossibly, it all works.

"Fifty-fifty on the puppy," Chase whispers in my ear.

"Ten-ninety," I counter.

"Deal."

I know he's going to show up with a puppy anyway. Probably next week. Definitely named something ridiculous like Zamboni Jr. or Slap Shot.

And I'll pretend to be mad for exactly five minutes before falling completely in love with it.

Because that's what we do. We bicker, we compromise, and we build something messy, chaotic, and absolutely perfect.

"For what it's worth," Mom says quietly, watching us with Owen, "you two are going to be wonderful parents. When you're ready."

"Mom—"

"Or puppy parents. Whatever comes first."

Chase beams. "See? Your mom's on board with the puppy plan."

"I'm divorcing all of you," I announce.

But when Chase wraps his free arm around me, Owen babbling happily between us, Rip wagging his tail at our feet, and my parents actually smiling at each other across the room...

Yeah.

I'm not going anywhere.

Even if he does come home with that puppy.

(He definitely will.)

(I'll definitely love it.)

(But he doesn't need to know that yet.)

EPILOGUE II

LATER THAT NIGHT

Chase

The house is finally quiet. Rip is snoring from his bed in the corner, probably dreaming about all the turkey he charmed out of Scarlett's parents. The dishwasher hums in the kitchen—normal, domestic sounds that sometimes catch me off guard, making me realize that this is my actual life.

Scarlett is already in bed when I come out of the bathroom, propped against the headboard with her laptop, glasses perched on her nose. She only wears them late at night when her contacts start bothering her, and I love that I'm the only one who gets to see her like this.

"Still working?" I ask, sliding under the covers.

"Just reviewing the copyedits on book seven." She doesn't look up, but her foot finds mine under the blanket. "My editor wants to know if the hero really needs to apologize three times in the final chapter."

"Does he?"

"Probably. He was kind of a dick in chapter twelve."

I shift closer, my arm sliding around her waist. "Based on anyone I know?"

She finally looks at me over her glasses, fighting a smile. "Chase Remington would never lock the heroine out of the practice rink."

"True. I'd probably just steal her coffee and make her chase me for it."

"Which you literally did last Tuesday."

"You love it."

She closes the laptop with a soft click, setting it on the nightstand along with her glasses. When she turns back to me, her expression is softer—unguarded in that way she only gets late at night.

"Today was good," she says quietly.

I pull her closer until she's tucked against my chest. "Your parents were... surprisingly functional."

"I know, right? They got through an entire meal without a single passive-aggressive comment about the divorce."

"Progress."

"And what they said..." She trails off, her fingers tracing absent patterns on my chest. "About me proving them wrong. About building something they couldn't."

"They meant it."

"I know." Her voice is small. "That's what made it so..."

"Scary?"

She nods against my shoulder. "I spent so long being angry at them, using their failure as proof that love wasn't worth it. And now—"

"Now you write romance novels and wake up every morning next to a hockey player who can't cook."

She laughs softly. "When you put it like that."

I press a kiss to her hair, breathing in the familiar scent of her shampoo. "You know what the best part is?"

"Hm?"

"We get to keep proving them right. Every day. Every burnt pancake, every deadline, every time Rip steals your spot on the couch. We just keep building."

She's quiet for a moment before she asks, "Even if you bring home a puppy?"

"Especially then. Think about it—Owen would lose his mind. The photo ops alone..."

She groans. "You're not actually getting a puppy."

"Forty-sixty chance."

"Chase."

"Thirty-seventy?"

She props herself up on an elbow to look at me properly. Her hair is messy, falling around her face. No makeup. That tiny scar on her chin from when she wiped out on her bike at eight—beautiful.

"I love you," she says simply. "Even if you're plotting to bring chaos into our perfectly functional life."

"Our life is already chaos. We babysit with a foam hockey stick and use Rip as a pillow fort."

"Valid point." She leans down to kiss me, slow and sweet. "But still no puppy."

"We'll see."

She settles back against my chest, her breathing already starting to slow. I trace lazy circles on her back, feeling her relax incrementally.

"Hey," I whisper into the darkness.

"Mm?"

"Twenty-eighty on the puppy. Final offer."

She pinches my side, but she's smiling. I can feel it against my skin.

"Go to sleep, Remington."

"Love you too, Calloway."

She moves closer in the bed, pressing her body against mine—a perfect fit, like always.

I trace my fingers along her hip, my voice dropping. "Owen looked pretty good on you."

She stiffens slightly. "Chase..."

"I'm just saying," I murmur, pulling her closer,

my lips finding that spot below her ear that always makes her breath catch. "We could start trying. Tonight, even."

"We agreed—" she starts, but her voice wavers when I kiss her neck. "We said we'd wait until—"

"Until you finished book seven? Which you just did." My hand slips under her sleep shirt, skating across warm skin. "Until I made captain? Check. Until we survived babysitting? We kept Owen alive for four whole hours."

She laughs, but it's breathless. "That's a very low bar for parenting readiness."

"Come on," I whisper against her skin, feeling her pulse jump. "Let's make a baby, Calloway."

She's quiet for a moment, and I think I might actually be winning this negotiation. Then she pulls back, eyes narrowed.

"Okay, fine."

I blink. "Really?"

"We can get the puppy."

I pause, processing. "Wait, what?"

"You win. Twenty-eighty split. You can get your chaos puppy." She crosses her arms, trying to look stern despite her flushed cheeks. "But no babies. Not yet."

I stare at her for a beat, then burst out laughing. "Did you just—did you seriously just negotiate me down from a human child to a golden retriever?"

"You're welcome. Puppies don't need college

funds."

I laugh harder, pulling her back against me. "You're brilliant."

"I have my moments." But then she pauses, studying my face. "Wait. Was that your plan all along? Start with the baby talk so I'd cave on the puppy?"

I school my expression into perfect innocence. "Would I do that?"

"Chase Remington, you manipulative little—"

I cut her off with a kiss, deep and slow, until she melts against me. When I pull back, we're both breathing harder.

"For the record," I murmur, "I'm playing the long game. Puppy now, baby later."

"We'll see about that."

"Oh, we will." I roll her beneath me, grinning at the way her eyes darken. "But right now, I think we should practice. You know, for later. When you finally cave on the baby thing too."

She wraps her arms around my neck, pulling me down. "You're insufferable."

"You love it."

"Unfortunately." She sighs, but she's smiling as she kisses me again.

And as her hands slide under my shirt, as she arches beneath me with that little sound that drives me crazy, I think about how this woman just played me like a fiddle—and how I couldn't be happier about it.

"Best negotiation ever," I mutter against her mouth.

Her laugh turns into something else entirely as my hands find better things to do than talk.

And somewhere in the back of my mind, I'm already planning which puppy to bring home.

She's going to love it.

Even if she pretends not to for the first five minutes.

The End

Up Next

CHECKING IT TWICE

Fake dating a hockey player for Christmas wasn't on my bingo card.

Clare Johnson's job is handling PR for the Dallas Stampede—not getting tangled up with one of the players. But when Mitchell Drake—charming forward, fan favorite, and very off-limits—asks her to pose as his girlfriend for one week in small-town Minnesota, she reluctantly agrees. What's the worst that could happen?

Mitchell's had six months to get over his very public broken engagement, and his family is done waiting. The last thing he needs is pitying smiles and whispered gossip. Clare is smart, sharp, and strong enough to hold her own with both fans and family—the perfect fake girlfriend.

But holiday lights and snowy nights have a way of blurring the line between pretend and real. Clare fits too easily into his world—bonding with his grandma, winning at pond hockey, and looking unfairly good in his flannel. The more time they spend together, the less fake it feels.

Full of small-town holiday magic, meddling relatives, and sizzling chemistry, *Checking It Twice* is a hockey romance about second chances and falling in love when you least expect it. Perfect for fans of fake dating, one-bed tension, forced proximity, and happily-ever-afters wrapped in Christmas lights.

Because sometimes the best gifts aren't under the tree—they're standing right in front of you.

Acknowledgements

Thank you so much to my sweet little family for always being a source of encouragement and endless love. I am so blessed!

A giant mountain of gratitude goes out to my lovely readers. You are the reason I get to continue bringing my stories to life, and I truly hope you enjoyed this one as much as I enjoyed telling it.

Thank you to my agents, Jane Dystel and Lauren Abramo, and my audio production team at Dreamscape Media and Tantor. You're all truly outstanding at what you do.

I feel so immensely blessed that someone as chronically introverted as I am has managed to find a girl gang that is loud, faithful, and just flat-out fun. I'm so glad we get to do life, motherhood, marriage, and all the things together. *Mwah!*

Other Titles by Kendall Ryan

Unravel Me

Make Me Yours

Filthy Beautiful Lies

The Room Mate

Dirty Little Secret

Dirty Little Promise

Baby Daddy

Love Machine

Flirting with Forever

Playing for Keeps

The Rebel

The Forever Formula

A Beginner's Guide to Forever

For a complete list of Kendall's books, visit:
www.kendallryanbooks.com/books

About the Author

A *New York Times, Wall Street Journal*, and *USA Today* bestselling author of more than three dozen titles, Kendall Ryan has sold millions of books and they have been translated into several languages in countries around the world.

Her books have also appeared on the *New York Times* and *USA Today* bestseller lists more than 100 times. Ryan has been featured in such publications as *USA Today, Newsweek*, and *InTouch Magazine*.

She lives in Texas with her husband and two sons.